Unlikely Soldiers Book Two
(Secrets and Lies)
By Deb McEwan

Cover Design by Jessica Bell

Glossary

Block	Accommodation block
Basket Weaving Course	Slang for time in a psychiatric unit
BRIXMIS	British Commanders'-in-Chief Mission to the Soviet Forces in Germany
Chuff Chart	A chart used to count down the days until the end of a tour of duty
Cookhouse	Dining hall for soldiers
Do one	Leave now
Full screw	Corporal
In-night	Cleaning rooms and communal areas in single living accommodation
Leave	Holidays
LOA	Local Overseas Allowance
Mess	A place where military personnel eat, drink and socialise
Muscle Buster	Physical Training Instructor
NAAFI Break	Coffee/tea break at 10 am
Other Rank	Private to warrant officer class one (non-officer status)
R&R	Rest and recuperation – normally granted halfway through a tour
Secret Squirrel	Slang for Intelligence Corps personnel
Shuggle	Shake
SO2	Staff Officer Grade 2 (in the rank of major, grade 3 is a captain and grade One a lieutenant colonel)
SOXMIS	Soviet Exercise Mission
Stand Down	A period of leave granted by a commander
Staff Car	A car provided for use by a senior military officer
AFB 2066	A5 size book used for reporting on lance corporals and below, back in the day

Chapter 1

On the fourth morning after the car crash Elaine woke with a start. She remembered the suicide note and her frame of mind while writing it. She was going to be OK and so was the old man. Mouse and Guy were camping, Jill loved her and all was well, except for the note. She wondered if it had been found and what would happen if it had. She closed her eyes and steadied her breathing, forcing the panic out of her system. Usually decisive, Elaine was unsure what to do.

Six Months Later

Mouse was enjoying her job in the Orderly Room. She'd completed her upgrading course, learnt a lot of new rules and regulations and was becoming adept at helping soldiers with their pay and administration queries. Like most people, she hated Monday mornings, especially after such a fabulous weekend. Her two roommates were away, one on a course and the other had taken a long weekend to go to a friend's wedding. Mouse smiled to herself thinking about Guy. It had coincided with his days off and they'd spent the weekend together, most of it in her room, totally undisturbed. Males were forbidden from entering the female accommodation so they had both taken a risk and would get into trouble if caught.

'Right, Private Warbutton, come with me.' Sergeant Dickenson looked stern, very rare for him and the first time he'd used her rank and name in ages.

'Where we off, sarge?'

'OC's office for an interview without coffee. Look sharp, girl.'

Shit! Someone must have seen them and reported her. Even though they loved each other and Mouse wouldn't dream of cheating on Guy, it would be all around the unit and she'd be branded a slut by the time the rumour mill had distorted the truth. It would also be so embarrassing having to stand in front of her Officer Commanding to listen to the charge. She knew it was wrong but most of the time she thought of him as an old uncle rather than a boss, albeit a smelly old uncle. God only knew how many of those skinny cigarettes he smoked every day. He seemed to enjoy the process of placing them in the elongated holder. His dog stank too. It wasn't a Labrador, the usual officer type dog, but a small thing with a squished face and probably some sort of digestive problem by the amount of farting it did. They were supposed to ignore the smell but it had all been too much for Mouse one day. The OC was having a bad day and was chain smoking like a Beagle in a nineteen fifties test lab. Barnaby the dog was wet and she nearly threw up when he let one drop. Apparently he was now on medication according to Sergeant Dickenson, but none of them had noticed any improvement. Mouse stopped reflecting and followed the sergeant. As she waited outside

4

the OC's office, she pondered what to say. She'd had her first major disagreement with Guy that weekend when he'd assumed that, if she was reported for having a man in her room, his name wouldn't come into it and she would take all the blame. Mouse acknowledged that she probably would do that but hadn't expected him to make the assumption, especially as he thought his career was more important than hers. Much as she loved him, this was nineteen eighty-one and no way was she giving up the Army to be the little woman at home. Guy had laughed and said he wasn't asking her to but it sowed the first seeds of doubt and she hadn't been able to get it out of her head. Mouse was fiercely independent following her break up with KC Cooke. Having discovered he'd had an affair and realised how controlling he'd become, she'd made her decision at the last minute and had jilted him at the altar. Much as she adored Guy, she was happy as they were and wasn't about to trade in her career to be with him all the time. Besides, he'd talked about volunteering for special duties. Not absolutely certain about what that involved, Mouse did know it would take him away for long periods of time. Hopefully, keeping busy would stop her from constantly thinking of him. As she made a mental note to find out precisely what these special duties involved, the door opened and she was called into the office. Dressed in her barrack dress of skirt, blouse, woolly pully and tie, Mouse had been told to wear her headdress. She straightened her forage cap and marched into the office as best as she could in her court shoes.

'Morning, Private Warbutton.'

'Sir.' She halted and saluted smartly.

Major Phillips avoided eye contact and was looking at the papers on his desk. So he wasn't smoking. This must be serious she thought before she noticed a smirk playing around his mouth. So he thinks it's funny, what a bastard. She wished some nasty events on him before he spoke again.

'Good weekend, Private Warbutton?' He didn't hide the big smile on his face and neither did Sergeant Dickenson. Mouse tried to hide her confusion as she answered the question with a yes.

'Why have you come to my office incorrectly dressed?'

It didn't click and she checked herself over. The OC and Sergeant Dickenson started laughing. She stood patiently as Major Phillips slowly placed a cigarette in its holder. Before lighting it he opened a drawer and produced a red lance corporal stripe.

'Go and get this sewn onto your woolly pully Lance Corporal Warbutton, then you won't be incorrectly dressed. And congratulations, it's well deserved.'

'Yes, sir.' She felt like she'd grown two feet as she left his office.

'You bastard, sarge.' Mouse was laughing and so was Sergeant Dickenson.

'Careful, Mouse. Unless you want to be bust to private. Now go and get that sewn onto your jumper, then go to the stores and get your other uniforms sorted. And I suppose you can have some time to phone that fella of yours and your family. Back in an hour and don't take the piss.'

Mouse had no intention of doing so. She was now on the first rung of the ladder and planned to go up, and not down.

'Cheers, sarge.' She'd phone Guy first, her parents, then see if she could get hold of her brother Graham. Graham was a driver in the Royal Corps of Transport and was currently on leave with his girlfriend Grace, who also happened to be a best friend of Mouse, so she could kill two birds with one stone. Or should she phone her other best friend from basic training, Elaine before Graham and Grace? Whatever way she looked at it, it was a brilliant start to the week.

A few days later, Mouse asked Sergeant Dickenson about special duties.

'Are you serious?' he laughed. 'Maybe sometime in the future, Mouse but...'

'It's not for me,' she rolled her eyes like a teenager. 'I want to know about it, that's all.'

'Why?'

'Just curious.'

'If that's how you want to play it, fine. I know nothing about it.'

'Oh, come on, sarge. You must know.'

'Tell me why you want to know then and I'll think about it. Is it for that fella of yours?'

'If you must know, yes,' Mouse folded her arms. 'It's something he's interested in. I've asked around and I've been given different info, mostly bullshit I suspect.' She explained that she'd been told that only officers or senior NCOs could apply. That volunteers had to be single and that they could serve anywhere in the world.

'Come with me.' Mouse followed him to the OC's office. The boss was out and Sergeant Dickenson went straight to the safe. She looked at some of the regimental photographs and paintings on the walls while the sergeant opened the Manifoil Combination Lock. She watched as he selected a pink folder, indicating that the documents inside were classified secret. A piece of paper was attached to the outside of the folder.

'When they need new volunteers, the OC tells me to include this on Unit Part One Orders.' He handed the paper to Mouse, which she scanned. The gist was that both men and women were required to undertake special duties of a hazardous nature in Northern Ireland from time to time, and that the training was arduous and rigorous. Volunteers were to be referred to a Defence Council Instruction classified secret, which was contained inside the folder. Mouse opened the folder but Sergeant Dickenson took it from her before she had a chance to read the contents.

'You don't need to know that, Mouse. And anyway, it doesn't give much more information except who those interested volunteers should contact. All I would say is that only a small percentage of applicants get in and for those that do I've heard that the training is nails – long and hard,' he smiled. 'Satisfied now?'

'Yes, sarge. Thanks.' She couldn't tell him that it had made her even more curious and that she hoped Guy would change his mind.

Her new posting came through the following week. Mouse was going to Deepcut, but not to the training depot, she was going to be one of the clerical staff at the transport squadron, opposite the main camp. She'd be further away from Guy but he'd told her he'd decided to do as many courses as he could before going ahead with his application. He needed to be super fit so was doing everything he could in the meantime to ensure his body was in tip top condition. Hearing his enthusiasm, Mouse knew this was something that Guy really wanted. There was no way she was going to try to stop him from fulfilling an ambition, so she decided to keep quiet about her concerns.

The time flew by and Mouse packed her kit, said goodbye to her roomies and work mates and made her way to Deepcut. Her new job involved administration for all squadron members. It was a tight knit unit and she quickly settled in and felt like one of the family. The OC was another older major and behind his back he was known fondly by the staff as Uncle Jeff. Mouse was pleasantly surprised to see that her platoon commander from training, Lieutenant Stratford-Pomeroy, had been promoted to captain and was the second in command of the squadron.

After a few weeks in the job she was informed that the unit's sister squadron in Aldershot was short of a company clerk. Her superiors, though she wasn't sure exactly who, had volunteered her services and Mouse was informed that she'd spend Tuesday and Thursday each week working at 41 Squadron Royal Corps of Transport. She had no idea she would meet a woman who made Cruella Deville seem like a kitten.

*****

Guy was waiting for details of courses he'd applied for. His OC put him in touch with a senior NCO who had completed a number of tours as an operator in Northern Ireland. This information wasn't common knowledge, but the senior NCO had worked for the OC when applying. As much as Guy questioned the man, he wouldn't give him information about the job or the selection process, but had advised him to improve his physical fitness. This he was in the process of doing and the OC had been great by letting him attend the courses he thought he needed. Guy told Mouse he wasn't expecting to get any time off for a while, so it didn't matter whether she was in Catterick or down south.

Chapter 2

Fighting fit again, the civvy police had investigated Elaine's RTA. The old man had admitted losing his concentration and veering onto the wrong side of the road. He was charged with dangerous driving and had lost his licence. Elaine visited him and they'd parted on good terms. Anyone who might have seen her suicide note must now know that she hadn't followed it through, so Elaine parked it in a corner of her mind, hoping to put it behind her and to get on with her job. She was posted to the depot and was delighted when chosen for accelerated promotion and informed by her sergeant major that they were looking for talented, tough, female soldiers for special duties in Northern Ireland. Knowing that Guy was interested in applying, Elaine decided to pick his brains when she next saw him. She heard he was passing through the following week, to be kitted out for some training he was going to do in Brecon. She rushed to the stores and caught him as he was leaving. It was tipping down so they decided to grab a coffee in the Corporals' Mess. After the niceties about life in general and a chat about their common bond, Mouse, Elaine broached the subject.

'I'm after some info, Guy.'

'I'm not working on much at the moment, but shoot.'

'Nothing to do with any cases.'

He waited.

'I've been told that I'm just the sort of female who might be suitable for special duties in NI, so need to pick your brains.'

From the look on Guy's face, he wasn't impressed. Elaine continued. 'Can you give me any info?'

'Not really, no.'

'I was told you were thinking of having a go yourself. You must know something about it?' Elaine leaned back in her chair and studied his face. The Guy she knew was usually more helpful than this.

Guy picked the green coffee cup off the saucer and took a sip. Elaine could see he was gathering his thoughts so resisted the urge to press him. She was becoming impatient then he eventually spoke.

'I'm still working on my fitness and waiting for a response to my application, but I do know that it's not for everyone, despite what the chain of command might tell you. You have to be tough, *mentally* as well as physically.' He'd emphasised the word mentally.

Folding her arms she replied, slowly. 'I am *mentally* tough. You of all people know that.'

'Other people's lives could depend on you, Elaine. I don't think you're up to it.'

'How can you say that, you know...'

'The note in your car. That's what I know.'

So he had found the note. She couldn't believe her ears. He thought she was in the same frame of mind that she had been back then. Didn't he know it had been written in a moment of madness and she would never do something like that?

'But, Guy. The investigation proved that he drove into my car for God's sake! He's lost his licence.'

There were only two other colleagues in the mess and they looked around when they heard Elaine's raised voice. She calmed down and took a deep breath. 'I was in a bad place,' she whispered. 'But even so, I didn't do anything wrong and I never would.'

'I'm not so sure of that, Elaine. And I can't let you do this when there's a chance you could flip and put others in danger.'

Elaine shook her head, incredulous. 'What gives you the right to be judge and jury? Eh?'

'It's my duty, Elaine. And calm down. You'll thank me for this one day.'

'I'm going to apply anyway, regardless of what you think.' She folded her arms.

'You leave me no choice then. I'll inform your sergeant major.'

'How long are you going to hold this against me, Guy?'

'That all depends on you, Elaine. I'm not sure you'll ever be mentally tough enough.'

'Bastard!' The other two mess members looked up as Elaine screamed the word and sprang out of her seat, almost knocking her chair over.

'I'll make sure that Mouse knows what a bastard you are too.' She stormed off. Furious as she was, she knew she couldn't tell Mouse without confessing about the note. She'd told her best mate she wouldn't lie to her again and here she was, almost being forced into it by Mouse's shit of a boyfriend. Elaine was

10

determined to get him to change his mind, but knowing how stubborn Guy Halfpenny was, it wouldn't be easy.

Chapter 3

It was Tuesday 8th September. Mouse had been in the Army over two years and it was a day she would never forget. Transport dropped her off at 41 Squadron at eight o'clock and she walked briskly to the Orderly Room. Having such a poor sense of direction, she'd had the common sense to recce the unit the previous week and had written herself directions, to avoid taking a wrong turn. Knocking on the door she entered without being told to and sensed an atmosphere straight away. Quickly taking in the scene Mouse noticed a civilian typist click clacking at the keys of her machine and, at a desk directly facing the typist's, a scruffy looking chubby male sergeant counting money. The male sergeant looked up and smirked then returned to the job in hand. The typist was doing her best to ignore the two women at the other desk. One, a female lance corporal was sitting down and the other, a female sergeant was standing, leaning into the face of the lance corporal.

'Stand up when I speak to you.'

She was obviously angry but there was more to it than that. Her voice gave Mouse the creeps and she knew straight away that this woman was trouble.

'Yes, sarge.' The lance corporal replied, standing up slowly. Something in the sergeant's cheek twitched and Mouse saw her redden as the lance corporal looked smug.

The sergeant slammed her fist on the desk. 'That's it. I've had enough of your insubordination. You should have learnt your lesson by now. But I can see you need a few more extras...'

The male sergeant looked up from his work. 'That's enough. Fay hasn't done anything wrong.'

'Nothing wrong? Nothing wrong! She's insubordinate and it's your damn fault that she has ideas above her station. You are so soft with these girls that you make the job harder for me and any other female senior that they come into contact with. If it wasn't for...'

'Don't be so dramastic, Moira,' said the male sergeant. 'I think we should carry on this discussion elsewhere.' Mouse seemed to be the only one who'd noticed his unusual use of the English language. He smiled at her as he stood up and she looked away as he left the office. The female sergeant followed him out, still ranting as she did so. She gave Mouse a look on her way out which gave her the creeps and Mouse knew she would avoid the nasty cow at all costs.

'You must be Mouse Warbutton.' The lance corporal smiled as if nothing had happened. 'I'm Fay Anderson.' They shook hands. 'This is Eliza,' the typist acknowledged her with a nod, and then returned to her typing. 'Sergeant Tug Wilson is our boss. He can be a bit creepy but you'll soon get used to him and he's easy to handle.' She frowned. 'The evil cow is Sergeant Moira Jones, known to us minions as Vic because she gets up everyone's nose. Unfortunately she's the senior female in the unit and abuses her position by tormenting and bullying anyone she doesn't like, which is basically me and a few of the other girls. I have a complaint in against her but I don't expect anything to change. I can't wait to get out of this place.' Fay explained that she'd been selected for promotion and was posted to Germany six weeks later. 'We're already undermanned but they won't stop my promotion and that's why you're here.' She gave Mouse a sympathetic look. 'I can't wait to leave this shit unit. Because I'm a clerk and turned down her advances, she's made my life absolute hell.' Mouse listened in morbid fascination as Fay shared her experiences where Sergeant Jones had humiliated her or picked on her in front of other members of the unit. 'I'm telling you this because you need to know what you're dealing with. What she calls character building, most people call bullying. If I thought I could win a fight against her, I would have sneaked up on her at night and attacked her by now.' Mouse didn't doubt that she actually meant it. She wasn't looking forward to her dealings with Sergeant Jones and intended to keep out of her way. Unfortunately, it wasn't that simple.

Later, during her initial interview, Sergeant Jones talked at her. 'We have parades on Tuesday mornings, zero six forty five hours.'

'Yes, sarge.'

'I'm telling you this, Lance Corporal Warbutton, because I expect you to be there.'

Mouse was confused. The unit knew that her transport didn't arrive until eight in the morning. She tried explaining to Sergeant Jones. The woman refused to listen.

'But, sarge, my transport doesn't get here until eight o'clock.'

'You mean zero eight hundred hours.'

Mouse tried not to roll her eyes. 'Yes, sarge, zero eight hundred hours. I haven't got any control over it.'

'Do you want to get on in the Army, Warbutton?'

Mouse nodded.

'Then you'll learn to use your initiative and follow orders. Understand?'

God, she was such a bitch. 'Yes, sarge.' How was she supposed to deal with such a bitter, nasty woman.

Back in Deepcut, she explained her dilemma. Her troop sergeant was helpful and decided to phone Sergeant Jones to explain that they couldn't get her to Aldershot any earlier on Tuesdays or Thursdays, because the duty driver already had a standing detail to Camberley early in the morning. There was no way he could justify another driver and vehicle just to satisfy Sergeant Jones. Mouse was told it was sorted so wasn't prepared for the debacle the following Tuesday.

As she was about to remove her coat, the phone rang. She was the only one in the office so answered.

'Why are you in the office, Corporal Warbutton?'

Because I work here. She resisted the urge, knowing she would come off worst from the conversation.

'I'm just in, sarge. How can I help you?'

'You can help by coming to the square. Don't think you're excused because you can't get here in time. March onto the courtyard square, stand at ease and await my orders.'

'Is this some sort of wind-up?' Mouse looked at the phone. Not even Sergeant Jones could be this barking. Surely?

'It's not a fucking wind-up, girl. Get out there now or suffer the consequences.'

The courtyard square was surrounded by buildings that housed the squadron offices. As Mouse marched into the centre and glanced up at windows she saw a number of faces, both military and civilian, staring down at her. She knew Sergeant Jones was deadly serious and felt totally humiliated. She'd stood at ease for what seemed like forever before hearing a voice.

'Parade, parade 'shun.'

It seemed totally ridiculous and reminded Mouse of something from a Monty Python sketch. She resisted the urge to laugh and run off the square. She brought herself to attention and watched as Sergeant Jones marched onto the square. *Jesus Christ! Was this for real?*

Mouse avoided eye contact and focused on a window, directly in her line of sight.

The sergeant looked her up and down then walked around to inspect her from behind. She returned to the front and stood in front of Mouse, frowning.

'You have dust on your headdress and your shoes need some work. Your tie isn't straight and your woolly pully is loose.' Following each criticism her voice became louder. 'This may be an acceptable standard for clerks, Warbutton, but you're in a driver squadron now and we expect better.' Her face was so close that Mouse could smell nicotine and last night's lager on her breath.

'Come and see me at lunchtime, or go in front of the OC on a charge. Your choice.'

Close to tears, Mouse bit her bottom lip. She wasn't going to let this bitch break her.

'Yes, sarge.'

Sergeant Jones gave a satisfied smile, then shouted. 'Parade, parade, dismiss.'

Mouse turned to the right, marched three steps then relaxed, as she would do on a normal parade.

'We'll make a soldier out of you yet,' said her tormentor before walking off the square.

Mouse made her way to the office. She knew she needed to talk to someone about the situation but wasn't sure how to handle it. Her visit to Sergeant Jones's office resulted in two extra duties and a warning that it would be worse the following week if her standards didn't improve.

Six weeks later and Mouse had taken to carrying in an extra set of kit for her Tuesday morning parades. It didn't really matter as Sergeant Jones always picked her up for something, even though her turnout was immaculate. Mouse was on the parade square once again. Her troop sergeant in Deepcut told her to *grow a set* and she knew it would look bad on him if she went higher up. Desperate, she decided to approach Sergeant Wilson. He'd initially told her he tried not to get involved with WRAC matters, that it was out of his jurisdiction and that she should try not to antagonise Sergeant Jones. That was a bloody laugh, it was the other way around. There might be light at the end of the tunnel thought Mouse as she stood on the square awaiting the arrival of the nasty bitch. Sergeant Wilson seemed to have changed his mind and wanted to hear everything. Pacifically – he had actually said pacifically instead of specifically – if any bullying was involved. He told her to stay behind after work that night to tell him all about it, and he'd see if he could help. Mouse looked around at the windows overlooking the courtyard. Her parade had become a spectacle and some of the drivers would stand at the windows and hold cards up with numbers on when Sergeant Jones wasn't looking. All tens today, just like the perfect Olympic gymnast.

'Yes!'

Mouse tried to keep a straight face and hide her small sense of satisfaction as she remembered when the bitch had gone apeshit, once she'd discovered that some of the soldiers were taking the piss. She was the one who'd received the bollocking, not the mickey takers. It was no good trying to figure out why she was such a bitch. She made her life too miserable and Mouse wanted to spend as little time as possible thinking about the hag. Today was Fay's last day at the unit and the squadron were having drinks for her after work. Mouse would have her chat with Sergeant Wilson while everyone else was at the drinks, and then join them in the Squadron Bar. Fay could be bitchy and was impatient with some of the soldiers who came into the Orderly Room, but Mouse got on well with her probably because of their shared dislike of Sergeant Jones.

Mouse wasn't yet ready to sit her driving test so the duty driver was happy to pick her up later that night. She tried to shake off any thoughts of the bitch by looking forward to Fay's drinks and hoping that Sergeant Wilson would be able to make her life in the unit more bearable. He came across as thick because of the way he misused words, and she wondered how he had reached the rank of sergeant. Hopefully it was because he was a good manager and could make a difference after all. She tried to forget about her problems for a while and focus on the good in her life. There was the long weekend to look forward to the following month when she was taking leave and meeting Guy in Blackpool.

By the time she arrived, the Orderly Room was empty except for Sergeant Wilson.

'Get us a brew, Mouse, then we'll talk in the OC's office, where we won't be boffered.'

'OK, sarge, but it's quiet here, everyone's at the drinks.'

He ignored her comment and made his way to the OC's office. 'Bring the brews in when they're ready.'

16

'OK.' Mouse thought it a little strange, but he was the boss.

A few minutes later she walked into the office with her coffee and a cup of tea for Sergeant Wilson. He was sitting behind the OC's desk. She couldn't quite place why, but he looked a little strange. Mouse put the drinks down on the small coffee table between the two comfy chairs.

'Sarge?'

'So you want my help, young Mouse?'

'Err yes, sarge.' She didn't like the way he leered at her and was starting to feel uncomfortable.

She waited for him to say something, but instead he stood up. She could see the bulge in his lightweights before he unzipped them and the trousers dropped to his ankles. He touched himself through his old fashioned spotted pants.

'I'm sure we can come to some arrangement, young Mouse.' His eyes were almost closed as he spoke and he was rubbing himself.

Mouse was disgusted. 'Not in a million years, you fucking pervert.'

He laughed and pulled up his trousers. 'Don't be so dramatic. A man's got to try,' were the last words she heard as she hurried from the office, slamming the door behind her. She was in two minds whether to go to the drinks, worried that she now had two people in the unit that she would like to avoid at all costs but wasn't able to. Sergeant Wilson was married for God's sake and his wife was a serving sergeant! These were the worst senior NCOs Mouse had met in her short career and she wondered what was wrong with people. Knowing that Fay would be disappointed if she didn't turn up for her leaving drinks, she put on a brave face and decided to go. She would report Sergeant Wilson to her parent unit. Nobody should have to put up with that sort of behaviour and Mouse hoped that he would be disciplined and she wouldn't have to return to 41 Squadron ever again. She got her wish but for all the wrong reasons.

Despite the incident with Sergeant Wilson, the drinks were a good laugh. Sergeant Jones spent her time in a corner talking to two of her corporals and they looked like they were enjoying themselves. According to Fay, the junior NCOs who were liked by Sergeant Jones could get away with anything. She'd given

17

her examples of one or two of them not getting into trouble for fighting or being late for parades. Had it been anyone other than Sergeant Jones and Mouse would have thought Fay was exaggerating, but now she wasn't sure. Fay went to the bar at one point when the bitch was there. Mouse had no idea what had been said but Sergeant Jones's cheek twitched like it had the first time she'd seen them have words. Fay smiled and winked at Mouse as she passed her on her way to talk to another group of soldiers. Tipsy, but still aware of what was going on, Mouse said her goodbyes. As much as she tried, she couldn't get Sergeant Wilson or Sergeant Jones out of her head, so decided it was time to leave.

'Keep in touch and let's get together when I'm on leave.'

Mouse nodded and after hugging Fay, left the bar. She didn't notice that Sergeant Jones was no longer there.

*****

Mouse unlocked her bunk and put the kettle on. She got into her scruffs then made a coffee. She was back at what she thought of as her normal job the following day, and with all the recent kerfuffle, didn't want to go into work hung over or stinking of booze. Taking her coffee she wandered up the corridor to the communal TV room singing *Tainted Love* as she did so.

'Shut the fuck up, Mouse, you fucking retard.'

Mouse chuckled to herself. Scottish English could be very colourful indeed.

The girls were watching Brian Jacks in the semi-final of *Superstars* and Mouse knew her arse would end up in a sling if she interrupted. They took their eyes off the TV to smile or nod to her but the room was silent, besides for the clack clacking of Mavis's knitting needles. There was a layer of smoke hovering in the air and Mavis gave her a dirty look when she got up, crept to the window in exaggerated fashion like a cartoon character, and opened it to let in some air. She sat back down quietly and joined the comfortable silence of her mates. The silence was broken when two RMPs barged into the room twenty minutes later. Mouse recognised the female from a function she'd attended at Guy's Mess a few months before. She wondered if something had happened to him on his course.

'Lance Corporal Warbutton?' the male asked, but the female recognised her too and whispered in her colleague's ear. He looked directly at her.

'Come with us.'

18

Mavis put down her knitting and turned off the TV.

'She's not going anywhere until you tell us what's happening.'

Corporal Bent knew a barrack room lawyer when he saw one. He would have been relaxing in his bunk for an hour if this call hadn't come in. Wishing he hadn't answered the fucking phone in the block he scowled at the woman.

'It's none of your business. We need Lance Corporal Warbutton to help us with our enquiries if that's all right with you?'

Mavis smiled and picked up her knitting needles. She knew there was nothing she could do but liked winding up the bastards.

'That's fine as long as you bring her back to us safely.'

They ignored her and motioned for Mouse to come with them.

'What's all this about? Has something happened to Guy?'

'Nothing like that,' said the woman. Mouse remembered the interrogation when she'd been in trade training in Deepcut and her stomach flipped. 'Get your shoes and coat.'

She did as bid. They refused to answer her questions as she sat in the back of the RMP car on the way to the station, feeling like a criminal even though she hadn't done anything wrong.

*****

Three hours later Mouse was exhausted and upset but there was no sign that they were going to release her.

'Why don't you just admit it? This will be over a lot quicker then?'

She was being questioned by two senior NCOs, a female staff sergeant and male sergeant. The female played bad cop and the male good. Mouse wondered if they were fans of Starsky and Hutch but resisted the urge to ask.

Sergeant Jones had been beaten up. Mouse wasn't surprised and hadn't helped her cause when she showed a lack of sympathy.

'I'm not really surprised. She's a complete bitch most of the time.'

'So you admit you're happy she's had the shit kicked out of her?'

'Err, hang on. I didn't say that.'

19

But it was too late. It was pretty obvious to Mouse that they thought she did it. She knew she was innocent so didn't believe she had anything to worry about.

She was wrong.

*****

Guy, along with a number of other military police, some logisticians and engineers, were training with the infantry at Ashford. The Northern Ireland Training and Advisory Team had set up the training area to simulate the conditions of the places the infantry were likely to patrol in Northern Ireland. Although Guy had already completed one tour, he had seen it from a military policeman's point of view, and not from a member of the Det, as the Special Duties Intelligence Company was known. He would have to go through a rigorous selection process before discovering whether he would even be considered for training. Today's training would involve a simulated riot where the infantry would be required to control the civilian population, CIVPOP, as they liked to call them. The CIVPOP were all soldiers, both male and female, and they had been told to make it as real as possible. This was nothing to do with Det's training but Guy wanted as much knowledge as possible to give himself the best chance of selection, so he had volunteered for anything he thought could be of benefit to him.

Soldiers were patrolling the area. A female pushing an empty pram started to cross a road. A military vehicle just missed her and she hurled abuse at the vehicle as it passed. Her accent was not authentic but, from what Guy had heard during his time in Northern Ireland, her words were pretty accurate. The near miss and her shouting were enough to draw attention and a crowd of people appeared, all fit men and women in their twenties. Some of the crowd carried thick sticks and had picked up stones. They started shouting at the soldiers and one of the men hurled a stone at one of the soldiers. The soldier with a radio called for back up as the personnel acting as civvies approached them. Some of the other CIVPOP had picked up dustbin lids and started banging them with their sticks. More objects flew through the air at the soldiers and, getting into her role, the female with the pram upped her screaming and shouting. She picked up a stone and threw it at one of the troops. The soldier rushed forward and grabbed her roughly and the other rioters ran toward the troops screaming and shouting. Most forgot they were acting and tempers quickly became frayed.

20

Reinforcements arrived and the soldiers eventually got the crowd under control. Due to the over enthusiasm of some of the rioters, and the response of some of the soldiers, the woman with the pram ended up with a black eye where a stone from one of her own side had hit her, and some of the rioters and soldiers had sustained minor cuts and bruises.

The warrant officer in charge of that aspect of training wanted them all to see how quickly a situation could get out of hand.

'This was an exercise and you saw the result. Imagine being part of the real thing? They always hide a few of the bad bastards amongst the angry civvies, so when our side is busy trying to calm the situation, they can try to take one or two of us out. You need eyes in the back of your head.'

The reality of the situation hit home, exactly as the warrant officer had wanted. 'Go and grab a brew and I'll see you back here in half an hour.'

Guy completed the training at Ashford and was off to do some more work with the infantry in the Brecon Beacons. This was to test his fitness and mental stamina. Although he was pretty confident about his fitness, he knew it wasn't going to be easy.

Chapter 4

Mouse couldn't get hold of Guy. He was out in a bloody field in deepest darkest Wales apparently. A part of Wales she assumed she hadn't visited. Elaine would know what to do. She contacted her instead.

'So you're telling me that this Sergeant Jones was beaten up and you're getting blamed for it?'

'Yup.'

'You didn't do it though? Right?'

Mouse held the telephone receiver away from her and looked at it. Elaine had to be kidding.

'Mouse, Mouse! Are you still there.'

'You had to ask?'

'Sorry. Force of habit. Of course you didn't do it.'

Mouse knew Elaine genuinely meant it. She sighed. 'I can't prove I didn't.' She explained that she'd left the function round about the same time as Sergeant Jones. 'Her bloody lackey said he saw me punching her, I didn't though, Elaine, honest.'

'And you don't have any witnesses to say you didn't hit her? It's their word against yours?'

'That's about it, yeah. She said I punched her and knocked her to the ground. He said he saw me running off and that it was definitely me, but they're both lying.' Her comments were met with silence. 'Elaine, are you still there?'

'Yes, I'm here. If the bloke is lying, she must have something on him?'

'Exactly,' said Mouse. 'I was told that when some of the soldiers in her troop have been in trouble, she's stopped it from going any further. I bet he's one of them.'

Elaine sighed. 'Sorry to be the bearer of bad news but if it's their word against yours, you don't have a leg to stand on.'

It was as Mouse thought. She'd been furious, annoyed and frustrated within the past twenty-four hours and now she was completely pissed off with the injustice of it all.

'What do you think I'll get?'

'I'm sorry but you'll probably be bust to private. I can't see you keeping your tape to be honest.'

'It's so unfair. I didn't do it!' In that moment she wished she had smashed Sergeant Jones's face to a pulp. She made a silent vow that she'd get the nasty bitch back, and Corporal Hoskings the spineless arsehole who'd lied about her. She knew there was absolutely no point in mentioning the incident with Sergeant Wilson because who would believe her? Mouse tried to get a grip of herself. She knew Elaine would worry about her if she ended the call this way.

'Thanks anyway. At least I know what to expect now.'

'I'll take some time off and come down to see you. We haven't had a good night out in ages.' Elaine regretted saying that as soon as it was out, Mouse would think she was being over-protective.

'It's all right, Elaine. I can handle it. I should find out tomorrow when I'm going on orders. I'll let you know.'

'OK.' She'd sounded completely miserable and Elaine knew there was nothing she could do to help. She wondered if she could discover anything that would tell her why Corporal Hoskings was prepared to lie for his sergeant. She'd look into it but it would take a while. If she found anything, it would be far too late for her friend, and anyway, the unit would already know if Hoskings was a serial troublemaker and would have questioned his actions.

'Try and keep your chin up and remember you're better than these people. And don't do anything stupid, please.'

'As if. Changing the subject, how's your application for special duties coming along? I half expected you'd be doing the same as Guy.'

There was a pause before Elaine answered and Mouse wondered for a moment whether the line had gone dead.

'It's on hold.' Elaine was glad that she couldn't see her face. 'The Corps is undermanned at the moment so they can't let me off.'

'How come Guy can go?'

'He's only doing some infantry stuff at the mo, and I wouldn't be able to do that anyway, being female. And it's because I'm a woman that they can't let me go. We have to have a certain number of us for investigations and other duties I can't talk about. They're never short of men but apparently this happens occasionally. I'll just have to wait for the time being.'

They hung up and Elaine was left frustrated that she couldn't do anything to help her poor mate. She was also concerned that she hadn't yet 'fessed up about the note and the disintegration of her friendship with Guy, and had already broken her promise that she wouldn't lie to Mouse, ever again.

*****

Monday morning and Mouse was at the regimental headquarters in Aldershot. Her case had to go in front of the Commanding Officer and she was waiting to go on CO's Orders with the other reprobates.

'All right, darling?' A cheeky good-looking soldier winked at her and she imagined he was a serial offender.

Mouse gave her head a slight nod, not wanting to get into a conversation.

The sergeant major called *Lance Corporal Warbutton* and Mouse knew it would be the last time she heard that for quite a while. She marched up the corridor as per the earlier instructions, feeling like she was heading for the gallows.

Inside the CO's office the charge was read out.

'How do you plead?'

'Not guilty, sir.'

'Lance Corporal Warbutton?' the CO sounded rushed and impatient.

'Yes, sir.'

'You know that Sergeant Jones said you punched her and she has a witness who saw you running away?'

'I know what they said, sir, but it wasn't me, I didn't do it.'

'If you didn't do it, then who did?'

It was a question that Mouse had asked herself on more than one occasion – she hadn't wanted to admit that her so-called mate Fay had done it and was happy for her to take the rap, but now she was certain.

The CO didn't know the accused or the complainant but something about the girl made him doubt the sergeant's story. However, his Adjutant and Regimental Sergeant Major knew the rules and he had no choice but to act on them. If commanders couldn't trust their seniors, the whole system would disintegrate.

'Do you accept my award or elect trial by court martial?'

Mouse knew it was their word against hers and even though innocent, she didn't have a leg to stand on. She hesitated and the sergeant major gave her a warning look.

'I accept your award, sir.'

'Very well. Reduced to the ranks. You're very lucky it isn't worse.'

She couldn't imagine it could be any worse as the sergeant major shouted. 'Private Warbutton, about turn, left, right, left, right, left right...' and she tried to make her legs go as fast as his voice dictated.

Mouse left the command corridor in absolute misery. So much for doing well in her Army career! She was told it would be a good idea to apologise to Sergeant Jones but received another bollocking for laughing in the sergeant major's face. That would be like admitting it. She was resigned to accepting her punishment but was far too single-minded and principled to admit to something she hadn't done. She'd already been told she wasn't working at 41 Squadron any more, so it wasn't as if they could make her life any worse and she didn't have to see that bitch, the pervert, or the liar again.

Mouse was determined to make the most of her work at 37 Squadron but was gutted when she returned to the unit and the second in command called her in. She could see by the look on Captain Stratford-Pomeroy's face that further bad news was to come.

'I'm disappointed, Private Warbutton, this is so out of character for you.'

Mouse recalled being in front of the head at school when she'd been naughty, only this time she hadn't done anything wrong.

'I didn't do it, ma'am,' she sighed, sick of repeating the same thing over and over. 'I've been set up because Sergeant Jones doesn't like me.'

As much as she wanted to believe her, the second in command had her doubts.

'We think it best that you start afresh elsewhere. I know you've always wanted to go to Germany, so here's your chance.' She went on to explain that they were short of clerks at the joint headquarters in Rheindahlen and that Mouse had been specially selected for a post in the personnel branch, General Staff Division One, at Headquarters British Army of the Rhine.

All Mouse heard was the posting part. She loved it at 37 Squadron and this was yet another injustice.

'So I'm being punished twice, ma'am?'

'Not at all, Private Warbutton. This is an opportunity for you to start with a clean slate and to prove yourself. I know you can do it.' She looked down at some papers on her desk, indicating that the interview was over. In case Mouse was in any doubt she added: 'Close the door on your way out.'

'I didn't do it,' muttered Mouse as she left the office and the second in command put down her pen and looked out of the window knowing that even if she was innocent, there was nothing she could do to help the girl.

As she packed her kit that night, Mouse reflected that so much had happened since Guy had been away, and he didn't know about any of it. As she was single, she was informed that she could be moved without much notice. Therefore they expected her at her new unit the following week, she could sort her leave out once at the new place. Mouse wasn't stupid and knew very well she wouldn't be able to take any leave until she'd been in the unit for at least a few months. She also knew that her reputation would follow her; the Army rumour mill would make sure of that. More determined than ever not to let that nasty bitch ruin her career, Mouse vowed to do whatever it would take to regain her stripe and get back on the first rung of the ladder.

*****

Guy hadn't had time to think about much during his courses. They were going through some new martial arts moves and the instructor soon realised that Corporal Halfpenny was more talented than he was, so he dismissed him. Guy missed Mouse so decided to surprise her by calling her office. He was the one who was surprised when the Chief Clerk explained that Mouse had departed for her new unit that day. He gave Guy the phone number of 29 Company WRAC in Rheindahlen and told him that Mouse should be there by that evening, providing there was no delay with the trooper flight. Having met Sergeant Jones on a previous posting, the Chief Clerk didn't believe her over Mouse and gave Guy his own take on events, assuming that he already knew what had happened.

'So she's been bust to private and posted, because you think Sergeant Jones and this Hoskings bloke lied about who assaulted her?'

'That's it in a nutshell, yes.'

'Thanks for that, mate. You're right. There's no way Mouse would have done that.'

Guy hung up and made his way back to the gymnasium, trying his best to control his anger.

*****

Mouse disembarked the flight in Dusseldorf and cleared through the section designated for British military personnel. The movers were well organised and it was a slick operation. She soon found her transport and joined nine others in the mini-bus to Rheindahlen. Seven men and one woman were dressed in jeans, t-shirts and jackets but the other, the junior officer, was easily recognisable in burgundy trousers, yellow shirt, tie and blazer both navy blue. He was reading a broadsheet newspaper. The bloody IRA had recently blown up a military vehicle, killing two soldiers, so for the time being all travel was to be in civvies. Mouse smiled to herself. It was pretty obvious, even to terrorists, that the smartly dressed man was an officer and that the others were military by the symbols on their t-shirts or their regimental rucksacks.

'Where are you off?' The other female on the bus asked.

'29 Company, Rheindahlen.'

'Oh, I'm off to 68 Squadron.' She went on to say that she was returning from leave and was a staff car driver. Her boss was the brigadier in charge of G1 Division in the headquarters.

'That's where I'm going to work!' They chatted until the bus came to a stop outside 29 Company administration block and Mouse made her way to book into her new unit.

'Afternoon, sarge,' she said and the stern looking sergeant looked up from her desk at the new arrival. 'I'm Private Warbutton reporting for duty.'

The woman smiled, introduced herself and gave her some forms to fill in. Thankfully she was really pleasant and Mouse relaxed while the friendly sergeant chatted. The corporal in the office told her to follow her and they made their way to Mouse's new home.

She was back to sharing a room again, but it wasn't so bad. There were only two of them in the four-man room and, by the look of it, the other girl valued her privacy. She had blocked off one side of the room with wardrobes, leaving herself a small entrance to get to her bed. Mouse didn't mind, if that was allowed she would see if she could do the same. She would, hopefully, be in this unit longer than the last so might as well make her bedspace and room as comfortable as possible. As she was unpacking she heard voices and a phone ringing. A girl with short, spiky hair walked into the room without knocking.

'I'm Spike, your roomie, and there's a fella called Guy on the phone for you.'

Mouse said hi and rushed to the phone. This was a bonus!

'I can't believe they've done this to you, sweetheart. Are you OK?'

Just hearing his voice and knowing he didn't doubt her for one second made her stomach flip.

'I'm fine...It's so good to hear you, I...'

'I'll sort this, Mouse. By the time I've finished with them those bastards will be begging for mercy.'

'Don't do anything stupid, Guy. Please. I just want to put this behind me and get on with my career. That's the best thing I can do to teach them a lesson.'

He was quiet for a moment. She had a point but he couldn't let them get away with it. It was his job to look after her.

'What's it like there?'

'Promise me, Guy. Please?'

'I promise I won't force them to confess.'

That was the best she could hope for and she was secretly pleased with his reaction, even though it worried her. They talked about her new posting and when they'd see each other again.

'I'll come over to you. Find out when your roomie's going to be away and I'll see if I can sort it before I do any further training.'

His earlier anger had gone for now, but Mouse couldn't believe what he'd said.

'Guy, I've just been bust to private and you want to get me into even more trouble by letting you stay in the female accommodation? Are you for real?'

'I just want to be with you, sweetheart. Come on, Mouse. We haven't been caught before.'

'Yeah and if we were, I'd have to take the rap again. I've got to go.'

'Don't be like that, sweetheart. You know I love you.'

'I love you too, Guy.' And she did, but she was still pissed off with him.

Returning to her room, Spike told her that she'd been assigned to take Mouse to her induction briefing the following morning, then to her new job in the Big House in the afternoon, and to show her around the massive camp that comprised the Joint Headquarters. Lying in bed later, Mouse thought about the events of the past few months, hoping to put them behind her and to concentrate on her new job in this exciting unknown environment.

*****

It was only a few minutes' walk to the cookhouse. Spike's radio had woken Mouse and they went to get their breakfast together. As she looked around while waiting at the servery, Mouse was struck by the size of the cookhouse - which was called The International Restaurant - the sheer number of people in there and their different uniforms. Spike explained that they were in a multinational military environment and that she would learn more during her induction to what everybody called JHQ Rheindahlen. Mouse opted for fried egg on toast and coffee. Carrying her tray, she joined Spike at the eight-seater table. The other six places were taken, the occupants merely nodded as the girls sat down. As she was eating breakfast, Mouse had the unnerving feeling of being watched. Looking up she clocked Fay Anderson. She wasn't sure who was the most surprised. Fay put her tray on the table.

'Mouse! Great to see you, but what are you doing here? And where's your stripe?'

Mouse recalled the conversation where Fay said she would have sneaked up on Sergeant Jones at night and attacked her, if she thought she could get away with it.

'Why did you do it?' The words were out before she thought through the consequences.

There was a flash of recognition then the mask came down. She was good thought Mouse.

'Do what? What are you on about?' Fay shrugged her shoulders and looked first at Mouse, then at the others sitting at the table.

Mouse calmed herself. Spike was listening but the others appeared disinterested. Even so, she didn't want them to know her business, especially when she'd only just arrived at the unit.

'What block are you in?'

Fay answered then changed the subject. 'But never mind that. You asked why I did it? What are you talking about? And where's your stripe? I thought you were substantive?'

'Sorry, Fay,' Spike interrupted. 'But there's an induction today and I have to get Mouse to the Globe. We'll both be in the shit if she turns up late. Come on, Mouse.'

'Can we catch up later?' Mouse asked.

Fay nodded. Before she had a chance to reply they both stood up and grabbed their trays to stack them in one of the dirty plate areas.

'Thanks for that, Spike.' Mouse hoped it was the last of it until she next saw Fay. Her false optimism was soon dashed.

'That's all right. You can tell me all about it on the walk up to the Globe Cinema, that's where they do the induction briefings.'

'I'd rather not.' She knew it was hopeless. If she wanted to get on with her new roomie she'd have to be honest with her. She needed Spike's help and knowledge until she settled in and the last thing she wanted to do was antagonise her.

'So what's the story?'

Mouse told Spike what had happened. She didn't mention her firm belief about who had actually assaulted Sergeant Jones, but it was pretty obvious to Spike from their earlier meeting with Fay.

'So, what are you going to say to Fay when you see her again? You obviously think she did it, but what if you're wrong?'

'I'm not wrong.' She explained the conversation about Fay wanting to attack Sergeant Jones.

'She's a full screw, you're a private. Get on the wrong side of her and she could make your life pretty miserable, even though she's not directly in your chain of command.'

Mouse knew that Spike was right, a lot of things could happen in the accommodation that would never get back to those she was to work for. Even so, after opening her big mouth, she wasn't quite sure what to say to her ex-friend. It still upset her that someone could do what Fay had and allow her to take the rap.

'I thought we were good mates.'

Spike could see her new roomie was upset. She needed cheering up before they got to the Globe Cinema and to work that afternoon. She didn't want everyone to think that Mouse was a miserable cow who came with a lot of baggage.

'So. Was that your fella on the phone to you last night?'

It did the trick and Spike was glad of the change of subject. She was also happy as they neared the Globe, having heard enough about *Glorious Guy* for one day.'

*****

The inductions took place every two weeks and the Globe

Cinema looked about three quarters full, so Mouse assumed there were a large number of personnel posted into and out of the location. They were told the purpose of the British Army of the Rhine was to defend Europe from the Soviet threat. The Commander in Chief, who was also Commander of the Northern Army Group, had over fifty thousand troops under his command to carry out this task. They were shown a video in which a big white building, the joint headquarters, dominated the screen. Mouse now understood why Spike had referred to it as the *Big House*. Following the video they received a briefing from the secret squirrels about the IRA and the threat within West Germany, and specifically within JHQ Rheindahlen. This was the norm for any new posting and Mouse struggled not to let her imagination wander. She snapped back to attention when the female secret squirrel sergeant introduced herself and told the audience she was there to talk about SOXMIS and BRIXMIS. Mouse discovered that the Soviets had a legal intelligence-gathering mission in West Germany and that the Brits and other Allies had reciprocal missions within East Germany. They were to be issued SOXMIS cards later with details of how to recognise SOXMIS vehicles, information on what they could and couldn't legally do, how to detain them and the telephone number to call to report the vehicle sighting. She gave a few examples of where personnel had used military vehicles to block in SOXMIS cars that had been discovered in restricted areas. Now this was exciting!

At the end of the main induction, senior NCOs from different locations took to the stage and issued instructions to personnel within their own units. The WRAC Admin Sergeant who Mouse had met the previous day, told all members of 29 Company to report to a room in company lines within the admin block. Here they received an *Orientation to 29 Company and Rheindahlen* briefing. They were told that JHQ was a town within a town and comprised some ten thousand personnel; military and civilians, workers and families. Facilities included a NAAFI superstore and a smaller NAAFI store within one of the married quarter estates, German shops and shops for other nationalities whose military personnel served within JHQ. A travel agent, two German banks two post offices, a dress shop, YMCA Bookshop, libraries and cafes. There were separate full British Army and RAF Medical and Dental Centres, four British primary schools and a secondary school. Most sports and extra-mural activities were catered for and the number of drinking establishments available was enough to bring tears of joy to any alcoholic. Their heads buzzing with information, the briefing finished on a note that they should beware of British and foreign soldiers and airmen who just wanted to sleep with as many women as they could. Any member of 29 Company found with a man in her room would be disciplined and risked losing rank, money or privileges, depending on how compromising the situation. Mouse looked around and noticed a number of girls looking down or smirking. So she wasn't the only one to think that this was like the dark ages. It was the nineteen eighties after all and women were supposed to be liberated – the Army could be so archaic at times!

Following the briefing they were issued with their SOXMIS cards and NATO Travel Orders, and told these had to be carried at all times, along with their ID cards. The NATO Travel Orders could be used while travelling through all NATO countries with the exception of France who had apparently withdrawn its troops from NATO in 1966. If they travelled over land and sea to the UK they would likely go via France and would need their passport anyway, so Mouse didn't see much point in the NATO Travel Order. She wasn't stupid enough to voice her opinion. The final document issued was the Ration Card. A number of the inductees were amused to discover that coffee was a rationed item and could not be bought without producing their ration card for the NAAFI staff to place a cross on. Once the card was full, they could exchange it for a new one. This applied to other goods such as cigarettes, whisky and gin. Those who owned their own vehicles would be required to have them BFG'd – registered with the forces in Germany – and would then receive a fuel ration card and be able to purchase petrol coupons at a price significantly cheaper than at the pump. So, alcohol was sold at duty free prices and was pretty cheap, those with cars were entitled to cheap fuel and all military personnel received an extra allowance – LOA – for serving overseas. Mouse would be better off in Germany as a private soldier than in the UK as a lance corporal; this was excellent news and a great start to her new posting.

It was lunchtime by the time the briefings and administration had been completed and Mouse met Spike as they'd arranged earlier. After lunch they made their way to the Big House.

Spike said they would usually enter the headquarters' compound via either the rear entrance, or entrance thirty-three which were the nearest to their accommodation. But she wanted Mouse to get a feel for the place. She pointed out the Rheindahlen Rooms, across the road to the right where various functions and meetings were held. As they walked passed a guarded entrance, Mouse looked at the thick steel fence that surrounded the compound. The imposing white building dominated her vision. They approached the senior officer entrance, and Spike explained that those using that gate and entrance number one had to be a colonel or higher rank, or accompanied by such an officer. As they were about to cross the road, a staff car pulled into the entrance driveway. They both noticed the red metal plate on the front with a star on it, signifying that a brigadier was inside. Stopping so that the vehicle could get through, both soldiers saluted smartly. Mouse caught a glimpse of the female driver who winked at her. It was the girl she'd chatted to on the transport from the airport.

'That's my new boss in that car,' she said, explaining to Spike how she knew. They carried on walking and entered the compound via entrance six. Mouse was overawed by the sheer size of the place and worried sick that she'd be lost as soon as she was left to her own devices. She daren't mention her sense of direction to Spike. She didn't know if her new friend believed her about the assault so didn't want to appear stupid as well as rough.

The usual administration for booking into a new building and security pass issue took place very quickly. The compound entrance was guarded by armed civilian security staff, and so were the entrances inside the headquarters. Once they were all set to go and had heard one too many of Edward the security guard's old stories, Spike dropped Mouse off at her branch, along with her bright new pass which she was told must be on display at all times. The grey haired, moustachioed Sergeant was the Branch Assistant Chief Clerk. He told her he was her new boss and her first job, as was usually the case in these situations, was to find the kitchen and get him a brew. He seemed pleasant enough and, trying to trust her instincts, she didn't get any bad vibes from him. Mouse was glad of the friendly face and hoped her instincts would prove to be spot on. The afternoon passed quickly. Luckily for Mouse it was a pretty straightforward journey from entrance six to the G1 Branch on the second floor, and from the branch to the female other ranks toilets. Spike phoned and asked what time she was due to finish and her new boss, Sergeant Waters told her she could go. She'd just finished packing up as per the instructions when Spike popped her head around the door. Sergeant Waters said goodbye and told her to be in by seven thirty the following morning. The Chief Clerk, Warrant Officer Class 2 Clarke, known as Nobby to his mates, was due back in office from a course in the UK and Sergeant Waters wanted everyone in when he arrived.

As they walked toward the accommodation block, they saw Fay in the distance. She must have left from a different exit and was standing next to a fence post, waiting for them.

'Good first day?'

Mouse nodded. 'So far so good. I think I'm going to enjoy it here.'

'You're lucky. G1 is all about personnel, much better than my job in G2. Now what were you on about this morning?'

As much as she now despised her, Mouse knew she wouldn't have a leg to stand on if she made the accusation so she just had to play the game. For now. She inclined her head for Spike to leave them to it. Spike wasn't happy but went along with it.

'I'm going to go on ahead, I've got to phone home, my gran's not well.' She rushed off.

'Did you hear that Sergeant Jones was assaulted?'

Fay feigned surprise. *And the Oscar goes to...* thought Mouse.

'No, really? What happened? I hope the bitch was hurt and scared.'

Yet again, Mouse found herself explaining what had happened following the assault.

'So you got busted for that? Surely nobody could seriously think that you would do something like that?' Fay was able to act surprised. She had sneaked up on her victim and attacked her from behind, in the pitch dark. Sergeant Jones hadn't seen her so didn't know who had attacked her and nobody else was about.

'Yes, but I didn't do it.'

Fay's expression changed and she now acted as if the penny had dropped. 'Wait a minute. You think that I would do something like that and let you take the rap for it? How could you think that of me?'

34

She did look genuinely hurt now, but Mouse could see straight through the act. Knowing she had to play the game didn't make it any easier.

'I didn't really think that, it was just a gut reaction and for that I'm sorry.' That should do it. Sorry about the way she'd reacted that morning, but definitely not sorry for pointing the finger at her so called mate.

As nobody had witnessed the attack, there was no way that Fay was going to admit to what she'd done, even if it meant losing a mate. 'You're a waste of space, Mouse. Keep out of my way or I'll make sure you regret it.'

Mouse looked down and nodded. She wanted to throttle Fay and didn't trust herself to say anything else.

'If I hear that you've accused me of something you've already been done for, you'll be deep in the shit. Do you understand?' She jabbed a finger towards Mouse as she spoke, to emphasise her words.

'Message received, loud and clear,' Mouse muttered.

'Now piss off out of my sight.'

She didn't need to be told again, but as she rushed back to the accommodation, Mouse wished she'd gone against the advice of Spike and had confronted Fay with the truth. It might have made her life more difficult but at least she wouldn't feel like a coward. She was surprised that Fay had kept up the act when there was nobody else about to hear, as if trying to convince herself she hadn't done anything wrong, as well as Mouse. Annoyed and upset, she wished all sorts of mishaps on Corporal Fay Anderson as she entered her accommodation.

Chapter 5

At 41 Squadron Lines in Aldershot, Corporal Hoskings was woken at five o'clock by two Royal Military Police corporals. He was politely asked to watch while they searched his bunk. They explained that they had his OC's permission to be there and that he had been implicated in a number of recent thefts. Corporal Hoskings was bloody furious. No way was he a thief and when he found the bastard who'd suggested such a thing, he'd string him or her up. He was the most surprised when the military police found a bag that contained money, watches and other personal items belonging to some members of his squadron.

'It's a set-up. I've been set-up!'

'Of course you have, mate,' said one of the military police. He'd heard it all before. 'Now get dressed quickly, you're coming with us.'

*****

Mouse had settled in and by the second week was starting to get an idea of how the branch was run. She had also become accustomed to seeing personnel of the most junior and very senior ranks walking the corridors throughout the day. Knowing she was the lowest of the low, as long as she smiled acknowledged their presence and rank by saying good morning or afternoon, they left her alone. It was different out of work where there were still in-nights – where they all had to clean their own rooms and the communal areas of the accommodation - and a corporal was in over all charge of the block. Her block NCO was pretty relaxed and Mouse was just grateful that she wasn't in the block where Fay Anderson was in charge.

In the office early one day during the following week, Mouse was surprised to receive a call from Guy. She'd given him the number on the understanding that she wouldn't be able to chat every time he called. He'd seemed bemused that she couldn't be at his beck and call whenever he wanted.

'I can't chat, sweetheart. Just needed a quick word before we do some phys.'

'Me neither. The brigadier is about today so the Chief Clerk is bound to be stressy. That's why I'm in early.

'I heard that Corporal Hoskings has been charged with theft. This proves what a lying untrustworthy bastard he is but we knew that anyway.'

'Oh, wow. I knew he was an arsehole, but not a thief.'

Guy quickly explained what had happened.

'What's likely to happen to him?' The rotten sod deserved to be punished. This was karma as far as she was concerned.

'Hopefully he'll be reduced to the ranks.'

'Good. That's made my day.'

'Bye, sweetheart. Speak soon.'

After they hung up Mouse wasn't sure how she really felt. So Corporal Hoskings was a thief as well as a liar. She wondered briefly how Guy knew about the case but assumed a colleague in Aldershot had told him. But why? Unless he was interested because of what had happened to her. That would make sense. Whatever the reason, she had a busy day ahead and there wasn't time to think about it now.

The social life in Rheindahlen was amazing. Although the job was busy there was plenty to do outside the office. If she left the headquarters from the rear entrance, right on the corner was the Euro Bar. This was the first stop after work on a Friday. Walking down the road prior to crossing to the Rheindahlen Rooms was the Belgie Bar. Following a few drinks in there, and depending on the time, a decision then had to be made whether to head left towards the bank and Teeks Bar, or straight across the road and right towards the Oase. This was used by the local and immigrant workforce but did wonderful authentic food and their spit-roasted chicken, sprinkled with paprika, was to die for. The main drinking establishments for British military junior ranks were the Marlborough (Marley) and the Queensway Club. The Marley was Army and Queensway Royal Air Force. Both clubs had recreational areas for pool, a TV and large disco halls. The weekend usually started by getting loaded up in the bars on the way home from work, back to the block to shower and change, then down the disco for dancing and more of the same. If she could still walk by the time the disco finished, Pops and Eddies were local clubs near the small town of Wegberg. The drive was a few minutes by taxi. The German taxi drivers drove like Formula 1 Grand Prix stars and Mouse often wondered if she'd arrived at either club, before she'd actually left the camp. Pops was on one side of the road and Eddies directly opposite. She'd heard there had been a few accidents over the years, of unfortunate soldiers or airmen being knocked down as they staggered across the road from one club to the other. If Mouse had forgotten to eat, the chips with curry sauce in both clubs were almost legendary.

For the first few months Saturday mornings were spent in a hangover haze, unless Mouse was duty clerk. If that was the case she refused to go out on Friday nights. Despite, or even because of being demoted to private, she was extremely industrious and thought it unprofessional going into work stinking of booze. She'd heard that the Chief Clerk had a drink problem and there was a rumour that he'd been on a basket-weaving course when she'd first arrived. Mouse didn't usually take much notice of rumours but did wonder if there was any truth in this one. After a few months she was beginning to tire of the constant partying and was glad of a break from it. After not seeing Guy for almost three months, Mouse was desperate to hold him. He was visiting later that week and she'd booked them into a small, inexpensive hotel down town. Guy thought it a waste of money but Mouse was adamant that she wasn't putting herself in a position where she could get into trouble again. She'd always managed to save and with the extra allowance from service in Germany, money wasn't a problem. She also knew that his male pride wouldn't let her pay for much so it was a win, win situation.

He still had his Capri and planned to drive to Germany. Mouse had been allowed to take leave the Wednesday, Thursday and Friday and was almost beside herself on the Tuesday night, while waiting for his arrival. He'd phoned when he left that morning and was travelling via Calais. He expected the drive from there to be approximately four hours so would be with her at around six o'clock. Mouse was all packed. They were booked into the hotel from the Tuesday until Sunday morning when Guy would return to the UK. He'd told her about passing his one day selection programme which had involved strenuous fitness assessments, IQ tests and an interview conducted by two men and one woman, all wearing smart civilian clothes. Guy had now been invited to undergo further training for a two-week period at an as yet, undisclosed location. He was to report to a barracks near Catterick and would be driven to his final destination from there. He hadn't been told what the two weeks would involve, just what kit to take, which he'd said was minimal to say the least. When Mouse asked for more information, he'd said that he had no idea what would happen after the two weeks, only that if he failed, he would return to his regular policing duties.

Neither Guy nor Mouse knew that events in a place that few people had heard of would drastically change their plans, and those of many others in the British Army.

*****

Spike crashed into the room while Mouse was waiting for Guy. She blurted out her news.

'The Int Corps people are carrying out an investigation in G2. Fay's in the shit.'

'In the shit? What for?'

'Some important document has gone missing. Fay's is the last signature in the 102.' The MOD Form 102 was a register for recording classified documents. They'd been taught not to hand a document to anyone without obtaining a signature. From the little experience she had, Mouse knew that if you handed someone a classified document without obtaining a signature, you would be in trouble if it went missing. Classified documents were more common in formation headquarters than in small units. In her current unit, each department had a storage area for these documents and limited access. There were so many such documents where Fay worked that most visitors weren't allowed in unescorted and all had to sign in and out of the Branch.

Mouse knew people liked to gossip but it was unlikely that this sort of news would be simply a rumour. If the document was really missing, Fay could be in big trouble depending on its classification and content. 'That's not good news for her. I hope they find it.'

'Seriously? After what she did to you?' Spike was surprised. She'd been alone in the G2 Registry and had acted on an impulse. She'd taken a risk by hiding the document and thought Mouse would be pleased at the news.

'Yes, seriously. I would like her to pay for what she did to me, but wouldn't want her career to be over.'

'Fair enough. So I wonder if this is some sort of pay back? You know, what goes around comes around.'

'Don't be ridiculous.' Mouse chuckled. It had occurred to her though, especially given what had happened to Corporal Hoskings. 'We only know half the story and anyway, how did you find out?'

She didn't have to lie when she explained that it was her turn to take the Restricted waste for burning that day. Two of the G2 clerks were there at the same time and were talking about it before they noticed they had company.

They were interrupted by a knock at the door and both girls stopped talking.

'Oi, Mouse. Your fella said to tell you he's outside.'

'Yippee!' she jumped off her bed and grabbed her bag. 'See you Sunday, Spike.' Running down the corridor and out of the block, Mouse launched herself straight into Guy's embrace.

'Am I glad to see you,' she said after coming up for air from their lingering kiss. Mouse felt the familiar tingle. This time the urge was so strong she could have stripped off and accosted him right there and then.

'Me too, sweetheart. Shall we?' She knew from the look in his eyes that he felt exactly the same. He walked to the other side of the car and opened the door for her. Much as she loved her independence, Mouse was so chuffed that the girls in the block who were rubbernecking would see that he knew how to treat a lady. Their time away from each other had seemed like an age. Although they'd spoken often on the phone, it was no substitute for being together. On the twenty-minute drive to Monchengladbach they initially made small talk. The anticipation of what was to come was almost palpable and the conversation fizzled out. Impatient with the check-in process, they had company in the lift so had to show restraint. Unlocking the door, Guy threw the bags on a chair and snogged Mouse, exploring her mouth with his tongue. She could feel his desire through her jeans and her body responded, passion hitting the pit of her stomach like a bolt of lightening. They broke apart and undressed quickly, feeling no need for words.

The first time was urgent and desperate, the second more leisurely. Guy was in peak physical condition and Mouse loved the hard feel of him when he lay on top of her. Putting her arms straight out above her head, she felt like her skin was on fire as he worked his way down with his lips, starting at her fingertips. Becoming impatient as he circled her belly button, she forced his head further down and cried out as his tongue teased her clitoris. He lifted his head when he thought she was ready and pushed himself into her, tantalisingly slow at first, gradually building up speed. All her senses were heightened as he moved deeper and deeper with each thrust. Their quiet groans became more urgent until they both called out and climaxed.

Lying together afterwards, without any words, Mouse knew that this was where she belonged. Wherever he was, she wanted to be.

Losing all sense of time they slept and made love, repeating the process until their bodies reminded them of their other needs.

'Shall we get some breakfast and do a bit of exploring?'

Mouse was surprised that it was already Wednesday morning.

The continental breakfast was laid out buffet style in the small dining room. She viewed the cheeses, ham, boiled eggs, various breads, fruits and yoghurts, while deciding what to have first. Opting for some fruit and yoghurt, she sat opposite Guy and started telling him about the brief conversation with Spike before his arrival.

'Two down, one to go,' he smiled. Looking pretty pleased with himself she thought.

'Eh?'

Guy stopped buttering his roll and gave her his full attention. 'Karma, sweetheart. Sergeant Jones is the only one left out of those three bastards who hasn't yet paid for her mistake.'

'Wait a minute. Is this your doing? Tell me you didn't set them up, Guy. Please.'

It wasn't the reaction he'd expected. As a corporal in the Royal Military Police, there was no way he would be able to make a classified document disappear from the security branch. But he had no sympathy for Fay Anderson after what she'd done to Mouse. As for Hoskings, the less said, the better.

'Guy?'

'As if. All I meant was that sometimes, what goes around does actually come around. If people are bad or stupid, Mouse, they'll be found out eventually.'

'Christ you had me worried there.' She kissed his cheek as she got up to replenish her coffee cup. Guy knew he'd said the right thing. He also knew he'd have to keep quiet about any future plans for revenge if he didn't want to raise his girlfriend's suspicions. Trusting she might be, but stupid she was not.

Following breakfast they explored Monchengladbach. It was dry and bright but the spring day was still a little chilly. The optimistic cafe owners had put some tables and chairs outside their establishments in the Alte Stadt and a few brave souls were there, drinking their coffee and smoking cigarettes. They walked along what some squaddies called the street of a thousand arseholes. Mouse could only imagine why! *The Gravel Pit,* seedy looking even at night, looked even sadder during daylight. Mouse showed Guy the familiar squaddie haunts along the street, places that she'd visited only a few times.

The time flew by. They'd discussed their future but weren't sure when they'd be able to see each other next. In their current situation it was easier for Mouse to have leave than Guy. They even talked about their long-term future, both knowing for certain that they'd found *the one.* The only concern Mouse had was that Guy seemed to think his career was more important.

'You'll need to leave the Army when we settle down, but it's a way off yet. I want to be at least a sergeant so I can provide for you.'

Mouse laughed. 'I can provide for myself thank you very much and I don't intend to be the little wife at home while you go away gallivanting, wherever the Army sends you.'

He told her it made sense for her to leave and silenced her with a kiss. His comments niggled, but she knew she could talk him round when the time came. They weren't even engaged yet, so Mouse didn't see the point of making a big deal of it, and spoiling their fun.

While they were away enjoying themselves, and unbeknown to the majority of the British public, the government had received intelligence that would soon lead to a war. Reports confirmed that almost the entire Argentine fleet was at sea and that the invasion of the Falkland Islands was likely to happen early morning, Friday 2nd April. The intelligence came from the interception of Argentine fleet signals and electronic code breaking from a secret establishment in England; there was no doubt as to its authenticity. On the evening of 31st March a decision was taken to assemble a task force. On 1st April, it was agreed to put troops on immediate notice. A number of personnel who received calls warning them for deployment and telling them to report back to their duty stations thought it was an April Fool's Day wind up. Others wondered what the Argentinians were doing in the North of Scotland, such was the ignorance of the Falkland Islands geography.

When Mouse and Guy returned to their hotel on Friday 2nd April, two Royal Military Police were sitting in a car outside. Mouse felt her pulse quicken, it was a military requirement that the Army knew your location when you were on leave so she wasn't surprised that they knew where she was. The surprise was that something must have happened to bring them to the hotel. Guy squeezed her hand and approached the car, their bubble had burst and something awful must have happened.

The visitors showed Guy a signal and quickly explained that he was warned for deployment to the Falkland Islands; he read it, noting that he was to return to his unit as soon as possible. They quickly packed and still numb, jumped into his Capri.

On the return journey to the camp, Guy switched on British Forces Radio. They both listened quietly as what the military police had told them was confirmed. Argentinian forces had invaded a British Overseas Territory some eight thousand miles away called the Falkland Islands.

Returning to work on Monday morning was depressing for Mouse, though she had some surprisingly good news. Her bosses had seen her potential and she was to be promoted to lance corporal. Acting not substantive which meant that she was on trial and could be demoted at any point. Mouse was over the moon and the good news lessened the sadness of being without Guy, but she was still extremely worried.

*****

Acting Sergeant Moira Jones had already failed her EPC, Education for Promotion course, three times. All NCOs had to pass the course if they wished to be considered for substantive promotion to Sergeant. This was her final attempt. Along with one other acting sergeant on the course her promotion had not yet been substantiated and could be taken off her if she were posted to another unit, if she didn't pass the test following the course. The rest of the personnel on the course were corporals from the Royal Military Police, the Royal Corps of Transport and the Women's Royal Army Corps. She had already singled out the two female corporals for attention and they despised her. Despite the course tutor's advice to the contrary, Moira knew that these corporals weren't her equal and while she had three stripes to their two, she was still their superior. Moira was embarrassed that this was her fourth attempt. She knew that if she failed this time she would go no further in her military career. Thankfully, her hard work must have paid off and the Education Corps officer told her she had a very good chance of passing. Moira was grateful and relieved; she had busted a gut to get to this point and had no intention of finishing her career as a junior NCO. She had always been good at the practical elements of military life, was reasonably fit and had therefore always passed the compulsory fitness tests. Her main failing was her academic ability and with this she struggled.

Three weeks later the sergeant major told Moira to report to the OC's office for an interview at fifteen hundred hours. She knew her results were in. There was no love lost between Moira and her new sergeant major, but she was desperate to know the score.

'You must know, sir? Go on, put me out of my misery.' Moira didn't show her feelings and it was a big deal for her to ask.

He disliked the woman standing in front of him and didn't trust her. A decent bloke, he knew about her previous failures so also felt sorry for her. But rules were rules and there was no way he'd betray his OC's trust whether it was good or bad news.

'You'll find out soon enough, Sergeant Jones,' his poker face gave nothing away. 'The OC wants to speak to you personally.'

'Yes, sir.' Bastard. She hoped his next one was a hedgehog. She left his office and decided to go to the Sergeants' Mess for a long lunch. The minutes seemed like hours and Moira was fifteen minutes early for her interview. The new lance corporal clerk passed her in the corridor while she waited. The girl looked down to avoid eye contact and Moira wondered if she'd imagined seeing a smirk on her face.

The OC walked along the corridor a few minutes later. She stood and saluted smartly. He told her to follow him in and shut the door behind her.

'Sit down, Sergeant Jones.'

He hung up his beret and sat at his desk, removing a piece of paper from his in-tray he put it in front of him.

'Bad news I'm afraid,' he looked directly at her.

For a split second she thought it was a wind-up and he'd say he was only kidding. His next words removed any doubt. 'You've failed. Again.'

'Oh, no.' She was gutted and temporarily forgot where she was. The OC watched as she put her head in her hands. He let her have a moment but coughed a few seconds later and she looked up.

'You passed at Army in the Contemporary World and just scraped through your Military Calculations. Once again you let yourself down at Communications Skills and, I have to say Sergeant Jones, that your Military Management results are appalling. The worst I have ever seen.'

Don't sit on the fence sir, she thought as he carried on.

'The desk officer at your records office is back in tomorrow. I'll phone then and let you know her decision. From my point of view I think it would be better for you to have a fresh start elsewhere.'

The careers of the WRAC personnel were still managed separately to those of the male soldiers. She nodded. She'd served under the desk officer, Major Jenny Winters in Catterick and had worked hard for her. Maybe she'd be sympathetic, but whatever happened, Moira was going to be posted from 41 Squadron. The only question was whether she would be posted in the rank of acting sergeant or corporal. She left the office knowing that the next day would seem like an eternity while she waited for her fate to be decided.

*****

A small detachment of Military Police who were part of 3 Brigade were to deploy with the main body. The planning went into overdrive and they all followed events as they developed during the next few days.

The task force departed from Portsmouth on 5th April 1982, three days after the Argentinians invaded the Falkland Islands. The government had apparently run out of ships and had to commandeer the beautiful cruise liner Canberra, which sailed on 9th April. Guy called Mouse to confirm that he was definitely off to the Falkland Islands with the 3 Commando Brigade Task Force on the Canberra, his special duties selection course would have to wait. As she watched the proceedings on Forces News TV, it seemed ludicrous that a luxury cruise liner was now home to some three thousand soldiers and marines. The man she loved was one of them, which also included paratroopers.

*****

The promotion had boosted her confidence and when the brigadier's personal assistant had been struck down with the flu, the Chief Clerk informed Mouse that she'd been specially selected

45

as her substitute. During her short time in the Army, she'd already discovered that *specially selected* generally meant that you were the only person available to carry out a given task. Despite this, Mouse enjoyed working for the brigadier. Her duties included maintaining his diary, manning his office and answering telephone queries, as well as typing his day-to-day correspondence. In addition, Mouse had to manage his *in* and *out* trays. She had access to interesting classified documents and, being in the personnel branch, what she liked to call *Oh Aye* documents, which could include matters of a personal nature. Very often she would observe someone reading one of these reports and remarking *Oh Aye,* after one or two paragraphs. It gave her an insight into what some people got up to in their spare time and made her realise that officers, who she had previously thought were whiter than white, could be as badly behaved as other ranks. Mouse tidied up some of the cupboards one day when the brigadier was out of office. She stumbled upon a case of an infantry major who'd had an affair with the wife of an Army Legal Corps captain, while her husband was away defending a soldier on Court Martial. Unfortunately for the wife he returned unexpectedly and caught the major and his wife in a compromising position. The major was fitter but still ended up the worse for wear. Mouse read some of the interview case notes with interest.

'*So, Major Jackson. How come you ended up with a broken nose and fractured cheek bone when Captain Little is clearly older and less fit than you?*'

'*It's very difficult to defend oneself when one is trying to put one's pants on.*'

She burst out laughing and read some more before getting back to work. On another day the Chief Clerk wanted to take a document marked secret from Mouse, without signing the 102 register. She refused point blank. The brigadier overheard the conversation from his office and chuckled to himself. This girl would go places. Mouse recalled what had happened to Fay. The missing document had been found by the investigation team. It was not where Fay had said she put it and, although no long-term damage had been done, she had lost the trust of her peers and seniors. She had been moved out of the headquarters and was now working in the Admin Office at 29 Company WRAC, opposite the accommodation blocks. Everyone knew that although she hadn't been demoted, she would have a black mark in her book, which would slow down any future promotion. There was no way Mouse was taking any chances while dealing with classified documents. Knowing that she was right, the Chief Clerk conceded and Mouse felt like she'd won a small battle. She was given the news a few days later that her promotion had been substantiated.

Mouse was one of the few military clerks who could touch-type. When the branch was given a new-fangled piece of equipment to try out, it seemed that she was the obvious choice to work on it. The arrival of the machine coincided with the PA's return to work so Mouse was allowed to play around with it, with both the Chief Clerk and his deputy standing behind her as she did so. She sighed, tiring of the many *wouldn't it be better if you did it like this instead of that* comments. Surprisingly, Sergeant Waters offered to make a coffee. She was over halfway through a letter at this stage when there was a sudden power cut. When the power returned, her work had disappeared. So much for the new-fangled technology! They discovered shortly after that a power surge had caused the problem. When anyone was working on the word processor in future, the kitchen in their corridor was locked, to ensure that a boiling kettle didn't cause loss of important work.

Another surprise was in store for Mouse. The branch was short staffed and she was being moved to the Compassionate Cell. There were five civilian clerks but Mouse worked for a corporal, staff sergeant and retired major. The branch was responsible for a number of issues to do with death and illness, travel of military personnel and dependants, and the issue of birth, death and marriage certificates. If civil servants or families of soldiers needed new passports, their branch sent the applications to the Consulate in Dusseldorf so had daily dealings with that organisation. She would have nothing to do with any casualty information from the war in the Falklands, as this would be dealt with in the UK. In addition, the branch was responsible for liaising with the Commonwealth War Graves Commission to ensure the upkeep of the military cemeteries within the British Army of the Rhine.

From day one Mouse got on well with the retired major in charge of her branch. Still addressed by his rank, Major Best wasn't everyone's cup of tea. He seemed quite normal to her and he dressed in relatively plain clothes, compared to some of the other retired officers around the headquarters. When she was new in the headquarters, it had been quietly explained that those officers retired from Arms such as The Household Cavalry or some

47

infantry regiments tended to be more posh or flamboyant than those retired from most of the Corps. Major Best had served with the Royal Corps of Transport so he was like a well-dressed version of men from her home, albeit still upper class by comparison. No purple or green trousers, or orange or bright yellow shirts for Major Best. He was also a consummate professional who was totally dedicated to his job, almost as if it were a calling. He could spot a bullshitter at a thousand paces and often clashed with Staff Sergeant Farrow who was her direct boss. Likely because Staff Farrow had a Masters in bullshitting, or so it seemed to Mouse. They actually had shouting matches. The first few times she stared in awe then later discreetly followed Corporal Roper out of their offices until the situation calmed. As Staff Farrow was also lazy, Mouse was on the boss's side. The good news was that he was due posting and would leave within the next few weeks. She wasn't aware of who was to replace him; they'd been told that it was someone who'd recently come off the promotion board and Mouse wasn't privy to that information, if she had been, she wouldn't have been so happy to see him leave.

Mouse went into work a little early on the day her new boss was due to arrive. She got a big shock.

'Hello, young Mouse I knew we'd meet up again adventually.' He smiled his leering smile and she was instantly transported back to Aldershot when he'd dropped his trousers in the OC's office.

'You've been promoted?' Even Staff Sergeant Farrow was surprised at her tone and Mouse was glad to see the smile disappear off Staff Sergeant Wilson's face. He gave her the creeps and she would try her damnedest not to be alone in the office with her new boss or working late at night with him for that matter. Once Staff Farrow left he would be responsible for the day-to-day running of the office on behalf of Major Best. Although Mouse knew that he could make her life very difficult, she also knew that it would be impossible to hide her discomfort and dislike for the creepy pervert. She toyed with the idea of spilling the beans to Major Best but dismissed it almost immediately. It would be embarrassing and she didn't have any proof. Having been posted to JHQ under a cloud, there was no way she wanted to be labelled a troublemaker or liar for that matter, especially now that she was back on the promotion ladder. She'd just have to box clever and avoid him as much as possible.

Life settled down in the office. Staff Wilson moved the desks together so that if she wanted to leave the office, she had to squeeze past him and there wasn't enough room to pass without pushing into him. It became a battle of wills and luckily for Mouse, her bladder seemed to be stronger so she could stay in the office without breaks, longer than Staff Sergeant Wilson could. Major Best didn't like the new office layout so changed it, despite protestations from Staff Wilson and Mouse felt like she'd won a small battle. Whether Major Best was aware of the atmosphere she wasn't sure, but was simply grateful that he'd put his foot down.

Although she loved her busy job Mouse was miserable, and her situation did nothing to take her mind off Guy. She watched the news and listened to any bulletins about the Falklands as often as she could. She was lucky in that although she received notifications about death and serious illness on a daily basis, none were to do with the Falklands conflict and she was able to compartmentalise and switch off during her down time. If she'd allowed the notifications that she dealt with in work to affect her, she would have driven herself crazy and, she often thought, be sent on a basket-weaving course herself. Not so with Guy who was on her mind twenty-four seven. Every time she started to imagine life without him, she gave herself a good talking to. It wasn't going to happen, he was going to come back to her safe and well. She had no intention of telling him about the pervert she was forced to work for. He had enough to worry about without her adding to his stress.

Chapter 6

The soldiers and marines were getting used to life on board the Canberra. Guy remembered that on the night before they sailed, journalists had held a sweepstake on how long Canberra would be at sea. Some had said as little as a week, others had suggested they'd be back in Southampton by late May. Nobody had thought the mission would go beyond Ascension Island, assuming that there would not be a war, and they would turn around and head home. Following the frantic days of assembling all the equipment and personnel, their training had started almost straight away once they were on board. The paras and marines were determined to maintain their fitness and started doing PT on the decks. Six laps of the promenade deck roughly equated to a mile and the journalists were woken at dawn every day to the sound of the troops pounding around the decks. At first, Guy and the other RMPs did their own training. The paras called ordinary infantry soldiers and Corps personnel *craphats* and treated them with disdain – because they were not para trained and therefore not considered good enough to wear the para maroon beret. Once they recognised how fit Guy and many of his colleagues were, some were allowed to train with them and Guy gained their grudging respect by proving he was fitter than most. The Royal Military Police were known as monkeys and members of the infantry taunted them by aping around. This sort of behaviour had long since stopped bothering Guy and he got his own back by telling the occasional infantry soldier that he was too thick to be anything other than cannon fodder. He knew he was wrong as he said it; it was simply banter. Although a lot of soldiers had little education, they knew what their job was and were ready for the task, even if they didn't necessarily agree with it. They realised that if they had to go to war, the way ahead was to go in hard and fast and to win as quickly as possible.

As the Canberra travelled nearer to Ascension, a feeling of real urgency spread amongst the men as they got down to the serious business of preparing for war. They attended various lectures and practised weapon training daily. Most could now strip and reassemble their personal weapons while blindfold. Marksmanship skills were honed together with the loading of rifle magazines and feeding of machine gun belts into the breeches of weapons.

They arrived at Ascension on 20th April and had a chance to march and practise their skills. The teams already at Ascension had built seven shooting ranges for the fighting troops to practise. Landed at the airfield by helicopter, they were marched the seven miles from the airfield to the range. The journalists were stunned to see the men, loaded with forty-five pounds of kit and weaponry, run most of the way. During almost two weeks at Ascension, the four battalions were able to zero their personal weapons and to fire their heavy weapons. The hills on the island made physical training more realistic than on the flat decks of the Canberra, which were starting to show wear and tear from the heavy pounding of the troops. Although the paras and marines had a reputation for toughness and violence, their antagonism toward each other was put on hold as they closed ranks with a common goal against their new enemy.

Journalists took plenty of photographs and videos, which were flown back to the UK and transmitted on all television stations. The British public followed the progress very closely and most forgot their real feelings toward Margaret Thatcher as patriotism swept the nation.

For those who'd not yet realised the reality of the situation, sighting of an Argentine Air Force Boeing 707 had done the trick. After the first few days at Ascension the routine was for the cruise ship to slip out of anchorage at night and to cruise elsewhere. HMS Antelope was near and started carrying out anti-submarine sweeps to ensure no one was below the Canberra

*****

Settled into her new routine, Mouse had been allocated a bunk now that she'd been promoted. Spike was still her best mate at JHQ although she was a little clingy and wanted to spend all of her spare time with Mouse. Despite being cajoled by Spike and some of the other girls, Mouse wasn't interested in going out that Friday night. She hadn't heard anything from Guy and didn't even know if the ship he was on had arrived safely in the Falklands. She'd heard that mail would be delivered at least until they were around the Ascension Islands, after that nobody seemed to know what was going on. Mouse had written him loads of Blueys - a forces airmail letter form three pages in length - never sure where they'd end up.

It was late and she was still awake. Lying on her bed, *All Creatures Great and Small* had just finished and Mouse tried to concentrate on *Instant German*, the programme on forces television that was supposed to encourage British soldiers to learn the language. The most interesting part was the parrot whistling to the music at the beginning. This might actually send me to sleep she thought as she felt her lids closing. A door banged along the corridor and Mouse assumed that some of the girls were returning from their night out. A few seconds later she was sound asleep.

At first, she thought she was dreaming. Then a vice-like grip around her ankle brought her suddenly and fully awake. Mouse had a fleeting thought that a smell was familiar. Very fleeting as all her attention was concentrated on trying to escape from the grip. Her assailant pulled her off the bed and threw her against the wall. She screamed as she banged her head. She had a second to look at him before he came at her again. Dressed all in black, her first ludicrous thought was that he looked like the figure from the *Milk Tray* chocolate advert. That thought disappeared when she saw that he was wearing a balaclava, and she realised there was something vaguely familiar about him.

'Leave me alone!' she screamed, terrified.

Without saying a word, he grabbed her right arm, threw her violently about the floor and set about her. As the blows and kicks kept coming she tried to give as good as she got, but he was much stronger. Now standing straight the man was breathing heavily with the effort. He put his arms to his sides and just used his boots. Each time she tried to move, he gave her a quick kick, as if taunting her. She couldn't see his face and he didn't make a noise, but Mouse knew he was laughing. Exhausted and battered, she curled into the foetal position trying to protect herself. She knew the only way to get him to stop was to speak to him, before she lost consciousness.

'Don't do this, KC. Leave me alone!'

He stopped. She knew without a shadow of doubt that she was right. Without saying a word, her attacker disappeared as quickly as he'd arrived.

Mouse managed to drag herself along the corridor, staggering along the wall. One of the girls was returning to her room from the ablutions and thought she was drunk. Until she saw the blood running down her cheek.

'Jesus Christ!' Julie ran to aid her. 'Carla, Sandra, come quick!' Mouse collapsed into Julie's arms. When the girls saw the state of her, Carla and Sandra helped to get her as comfortable as they could and Julie ran to call for medical and police assistance.

Mouse told the police everything she remembered, but not the name of her attacker. There was no way she could prove it and he hadn't left any evidence. Knowing him as she did, he would have an alibi and she would be made out to be a liar yet again. She recalled her wedding day when she'd left it until the last minute and had jilted him at the altar. She knew this was his way of repaying her and she didn't deserve it, after all it was KC who had been unfaithful. He had been controlling when they were together but never violent so she'd had a very lucky escape. Mouse was determined to get him back in her own way, she just didn't know how yet. But she would find an opportunity and he'd be sorry. Very sorry.

Chapter 7

Graham, Mouse's brother, received a message to report to his unit Admin Office and did so at NAAFI Break. The clerk told him that a message had been received from his sister asking him to call her at lunchtime. The hours between ten-thirty and twelve-thirty dragged. He knew something was wrong and wracked his brain. Much as he tried he couldn't concentrate on anything else. Graham's Troop Sergeant let him use the office phone and he called the number given.

They'd kept her in the military hospital at Wegberg overnight for observation. Although she was stiff and in some pain, most of her wounds were superficial so she was able to move about. She'd laughed when the doctor told her she'd been lucky but was glad she was being discharged later that day, though she'd be off work for the rest of the week and would have to get the all clear from the Med Centre prior to returning the following week.

Mouse was dressed, ready to leave the hospital as soon as the doctor gave her permission. She'd given the phone number in the lobby so made her way there in plenty of time to answer it. She picked up the receiver on the first ring.

'Mouse? What the hell's going on? Are you OK?' Graham sounded frantic.

'Calm down. I'm fine...now.'

He sighed deeply. 'What's...'

'I was attacked last night...No, don't interrupt, Graham, let me explain.'

She told him what had happened. 'They've kept me in overnight as a precautionary measure.'

'Is that what the doctor said?'

'Yes, exactly. I've got some cuts and deep bruising, but nothing's broken, thankfully. They thought my cheekbone was fractured initially, but it's OK. Honestly, I'm fine. They're discharging me today.'

'Who did this to you?' Although she'd told him her attacker couldn't be identified because of his disguise, Graham knew his sister well enough to know that she was holding something back.

'You know who did this. Don't you?'

'You should be a detective, not a driver,' she laughed. 'Yes I do.'

'KC.' They both said at the same time.

'I didn't even know he was in Germany. I'm going to string him up by the nuts and...'

'Graham, calm down. Please. I didn't know he was in Germany either. Can you find out from someone in your LAD?'

The Light Aid Detachment was the vehicle workshop where the REME mechanics worked to ensure that all the squadron's vehicles were in good working order. Mouse hoped that somebody in Graham's LAD would know KC.

'Of course. What did the police say? It's going to be difficult for them to charge him if you didn't have any witnesses. You know it's your word against his, don't you?'

'Yes, of course. That's why I didn't tell them.' Mouse moved the receiver away from her ear as her brother went off on one, ranting that she should have told the military police. She knew he was angry and frustrated because he just wanted to batter KC and make sure she was safe, and he could do neither.

'This is what he wants me to do, Graham,' she said when he finally calmed down. 'He knows that I know, but if I tell the truth and it can't be proved, he'll twist it somehow and my name will be blackened. I'm not going to play his games. I had a visit this morning and was told the security in the block is going to be tightened, so there's no way he'll come back. And anyway, you know what a bloody coward he is.'

Graham nodded to himself. He didn't like what his sister said, but knew she was right. 'What are you going to do when you find out where he is?'

'I don't know yet, but I'll let you know. I promise I won't do anything stupid.'

'Your idea of stupid and mine are two totally different things, Mouse.'

'I know, but I'll keep you informed. OK?' She didn't wait for an answer. 'And in the meantime, don't mention it to Mam or Dad. I don't want them worrying about me when there's nothing they can do.'

Graham agreed. 'I'm going to tell Grace though, and by the way, she's got some news for you but I'll let her tell you.'

'She's not pregnant is she?'

'Hell, no!'

'Are you two getting married?'

Graham laughed. His sister's natural nosiness had returned to the fore and this told him that she was fine.

'No. As I said, I'll let Grace tell you. I'll call you at the block later, when I've got some information for you.'

They arranged a time then hung up. Mouse was discharged shortly after. Her mates rallied round. They must have known she'd feel jittery about going back to the block and the bunk where the attack took place. It was as if they'd arranged a rota to look after her. Mouse thought she'd have trouble sleeping that first night, but with the help of her friends and strong painkillers, she was out of it before nine o'clock.

Grace phoned the following day, after expressing her concern and worry about the attack, she gave Mouse the good news that she was being posted to Germany in a few months. It was at least a couple of hours drive north of JHQ, but Mouse was delighted that she'd be able to get together with her friend during the weekends they were both off. She hoped the Falklands War would be over by then, but if not, it would help having one of her best mates in the same country.

When Graham phoned later, he gave her the news about KC. 'Bad news, Mouse. He's posted to the REME unit at Ayrshire Barracks. Is that near you?'

Mouse explained that it was in Monchengladbach, about a twenty-minute drive from her location.

'But he's not due there until next week so I assume he was on leave in the UK when you were attacked.'

Mouse picked up on his sarcasm and was glad that she hadn't given the police details of her attacker. 'Hmm. I think I did the right thing.'

'What are you going to do?'

'No idea at the mo. But when I do decide, Graham, you'll be the first to know. I can't seem to concentrate on much else other than Guy. I hope he's OK out there. And the rest of them.'

*****

At the beginning of May, troops on aboard the Canberra were given the news of the sinking of the Argentine Cruiser, General Belgrano. Their euphoria quickly turned to introspection when it became known that hundreds had died and the realisation sunk in that it could have been them. The mood changed again when they heard during the evening of 4th May, of the loss of HMS

Sheffield. Any previous sympathy for the enemy quickly changed to a need for revenge and the troops were itching for a fight. They had a little longer to wait. On 19th May some were moved from the Canberra onto the landing ships in preparation. They enjoyed a meal of steak on 20th May before the Canberra anchored in St Carlos Waters on the 21st; where the task force troops would go ashore. Some members of the special forces had already gone ashore and were directing fire towards various enemy targets. All the troops knew that they were as vulnerable as sitting ducks while travelling ashore in the landing craft. As soon as they were close enough they jumped off the craft in organised fashion and made their way inland. Those ashore felt relief whilst those left on board the ships waited nervously, feeling as if they were living on borrowed time. The first air raid warning came at seven hundred hours and by the time of the first attack at eight forty five their nerves were frayed. A number of ships were hit but HMS Ardent was massacred. Onlookers watched in horror as ten bombs were dropped on her during seventeen airstrikes, which Guy later discovered killed twenty-two of her crew. That day would stay with Guy and many others for the rest of their lives. He watched the ships being bombed, wishing that he could have accompanied the infantry, but it wasn't to be. His orders, along with the other military police, were to remain in the vicinity of San Carlos Waters.

As the infantry marched to war, Guy and the other RMPs were kept busy under the orders of his OC, Captain McDonald, who was affectionately known as Captain Mac to his troops. He'd come up through the ranks and had recently been appointed in post. Captain Mac had been Guy's sergeant major in a previous posting so they knew each other well and Guy liked and respected his boss.

There was a very good reason that the San Carlos Waters were now known as *Bomb Alley*. It was impossible to ignore the airstrikes as Guy came ashore with his colleagues, but they had to do their job to the best of their ability. The military police set up an information post at the beach and were given the task of directing troops to where they should be. It was organised chaos but the pieces of the puzzle started to fit together as the airstrikes kept coming. The brave helicopter pilots had to bring essential supplies through *Bomb Alley* and it was the job of the Royal Military Police to marshal the helicopters so that supplies reached their destination. This could only be achieved during the eight hours of daylight, all the while being under attack from the Argentine air force. It took all of Guy's reserve to concentrate on the job in hand and not to worry about being hit. He decided to let fate do its job while he did his.

On the 8th June, Guy was one of two corporals told to accompany the OC and sergeant major to Fitzroy and Bluff Cove. They had to discuss the practicalities of setting up a prisoner-of-war cage. They returned to San Carlos to the devastating news that the task force ships Sir Galahad and Sir Tristram had been bombed. Even though they were at war, it was a total shock as they watched the burning ships and prayed silently for those who were lost and injured.

Less than a week later Argentina surrendered and the war was over. There was mass relief, but new headaches for the Royal Military Police detachment.

*****

It was over. Well, the war part of it anyway. Elaine had been in touch to tell Mouse that Guy was safe, so were all the other RMPs. Two hundred and fifty five British servicemen had been killed; husbands, sons, fathers, brothers, their families and friends would never be the same again.

But her man was safe and well, that was the good news for Mouse. The bad was that she wouldn't see him for at least another two months. Six months! The longest they'd ever been apart. Elaine was going to come over for a weekend while he was still away. She was going to Spain for a week with Jill so it would be after that. She couldn't confirm dates yet but had sounded serious when she'd said she had something to tell her. Mouse couldn't for the life of her think what it was but didn't ponder too much, assuming that if it was bad news, Elaine would have told her by now.

They were going to organise it so that Grace would have the same weekend off. Mouse was so excited about getting together with her two best mates from basic training. They were coming to Rheindahlen and she'd be able to get them accommodation. She knew it would be a great weekend.

Now that the war was over and Guy was safe, Mouse wanted to concentrate on another matter before her friends visited. She had a bit of digging to do.

Knowing she was taking a risk, she phoned the Admin Office of the Rhine Area Workshop at Ayrshire Barracks. She introduced herself and started the spiel that she'd practised.

'I have a compassionate case for a soldier called Cooke. The family weren't absolutely sure of the location. Do you have anyone by that name in your unit?'

Quite often, relatives of soldiers didn't know the unit their soldier was stationed, so the clerk had no reason to doubt what Mouse was saying. He went away to check. On return he confirmed that Lance Corporal Cooke worked in the workshop.

'Is the comp case for him or his wife?'

His wife. WTF! Mouse did her best to hide her surprise. 'Err, where are they quartered?'

'Not sure, but what's that got to do with the case?' he didn't wait for an answer. 'Actually, they're moving to Wickrath, so...'

'Sorry.' Mouse interrupted. 'My mate's getting married shortly and asked me to find out about the married quarters. That was very unprofessional of me. Can you give me Corporal Cooke's regimental number please?'

The clerk tutted and shook his head. *Bloody women soldiers. If he had his way, they'd all be sacked.* He gave her the information and Mouse pretended to check the details.

'Ah. It's not your man. This one has a totally different reggy number. Sorry about that.'

'That's all right, love. Nothing better to do anyway.'

Sarky sod. Thought Mouse. 'Actually,' she said sweetly. 'If you've nothing better to do, could you send us the up-to-date list of your silent hours contacts, please? The one in our office is at least twelve months old.'

'Will do.' He replied, all helpful again knowing that he would be in the shit if she phoned his boss.

Mouse soon realised that she wasn't alone as she hung up the phone. Staff Sergeant Wilson was looking at her. She wasn't sure about how much of the conversation he'd actually heard.

'What was all that about?'

'I'm updating the contact lists, staff. Just making a couple of calls.'

'No, before that?'

'Oh, nothing, staff. Just made a little mistake that's all.' She blushed. 'No harm done.'

Probably caught her talking dirty to a soldier while her fella's away, he thought as he leered at her.

'Fancy a brew, staff?' She hurried to the kitchen as quickly as she could.

*****

Wickrath village was a twenty-minute drive from JHQ. The Ministry of Defence rented a number of flats from the German authorities to accommodate some of the military personnel and their families who couldn't be housed within the Rheindahlen military complex. It was one of what was known as a JHQ satellite. There were a number of them in the Monchengladbach area. The married personnel occupying less important positions, and who were less likely to be called out during silent hours, were housed in these satellite areas.

It was a Saturday afternoon and Mouse had picked this time to recce the Wickrath area, as she hoped that KC would either be playing, or watching football. She parked her small car in a communal car park and looked across the road. From where she was standing, she could see eight blocks of flats so Mouse walked along the path to the first one. There were kids outside playing, and as she walked past them, she saw a few of the wives, smoking and chatting. One nodded to Mouse as she went by and she smiled in response. She walked to the end of the first path until she came to the first block and noticed that there were nameplates alongside the door. Excellent. As she scanned the names, a woman's voice asked if she could help.

'No thanks. I'm looking for a mate and want to surprise her.'

'What's her name?'

'Ah, now that would be telling, wouldn't it? said Mouse, laughing.

'Well,' said the woman, studying her. 'You don't look like an Irish terrorist to me, so I suppose it's OK.' She pulled the main door behind her and walked back along the path. Mouse followed behind her shortly after. The two women who had been smoking were now chatting and she heard snatches of their conversation as she approached.

'They say he keeps her locked in the flat, and goes with her even to do the shopping.'

The other woman shook her head. 'Disgusting in this day and age, but she says she's happy and doesn't want to do anything about it.'

Mouse took a chance. 'Sorry, couldn't help overhearing. That must be KC Cooke you're talking about? My fella was telling me about him.'

'Is that right, you nosey cow?' But she laughed as she folded her arms. 'It's a damn shame, but she won't leave him. Too frightened I reckon.'

Mouse chatted to them for a few minutes. When one of them asked how her fella knew KC she lied again and told them that they'd worked together before KC had moved jobs.

'You must know that he doesn't have many friends then. Only bastards exactly like him.'

'Yeah, I'd heard that.'

'What brings you here then?'

For God's sake. This woman was as nosey as she was. 'They're talking about us getting a quarter here if we get married. He's on exercise so I thought I'd come and have a look.'

The women talked about the local area, telling Mouse where the NAAFI and military bar were located.

'There's a mixture of RAF and Army people here, but we all get on all right. Except for the odd one or two.'

'Where does he live? I wouldn't want to be anywhere near there.'

It worked like a dream and Mouse left shortly after, armed with the address of KC and the knowledge that his wife's name was Gloria.

It was a Bank Holiday the following Thursday and Mouse was off work. She was going to be on duty at the weekend so hadn't taken the Friday off as well, like some of her friends. She knew that the transport squadron was not on stand down, so took a chance that KC might be working. Mouse got up early and drove to Wickrath. Parking again in the communal car park, she made her way to Handel Strasse. KC's flat was number 3/8, in the third block along the path. She opened the main door and climbed the three sets of stairs to the top floor. There were boots and shoes on the mucky doormat outside the flat on the left-hand side, and the door had scuff marks towards the bottom. The doormat at the right-hand side flat was pristine and so was the front door. Mouse knew that was KC's flat and put her ear against the door. She couldn't hear a thing. She decided to take a chance and rang the buzzer.

'Hello. Who is it?' A timid female voice answered.

'I've just come to ask you something. Do you have a few minutes? She called back.

'Mouse? Mouse Warbutton? Is that you?' The voice answered and Mouse heard the sound of a chain. The door opened a little and she could see only the head of the small woman as she peeked around the door.

'He said you were finished and that he really loved me, I'm sorry, Mouse if he was lying. I...'

'Gloria? Is that you?'

The small woman nodded and started crying. Mouse recognised her as the shy girl from basic training. She tried to placate her.

'We are finished, Gloria. Ages ago.' He was obviously out because she was still standing there. 'Any chance I can come in?'

'NO!' Mouse nearly jumped. 'If he knew you'd been here, or anybody else for that matter, he'd bloody kill me.' She was whispering now and glancing at the door opposite as she spoke. 'You don't know what it's like. I'm almost a prisoner in my own home.'

'Why don't you leave him?'

'Huh. If only it were that simple. He's taken my passport and I don't have any money. If I escaped and he ever found me he'd kill me.'

'Let me in, Gloria and we can talk. I'm sure I can help you, or get help for you at the very least.'

Gloria looked like she was considering her words so Mouse shoved her foot in the door, trying to encourage her to open it. It was a bad move.

'No, you're not coming in.'

'Let me help, Gloria. Please?'

No response.

'I'm going to keep coming back until you let me help you. I can get you a new passport without him knowing.'

'Wait here.' Gloria closed the door but returned a few seconds later with pen and paper. 'Write your number on this and I'll call you. Don't breathe a word of this. If he finds out...'

She swallowed and the look on her face told Mouse everything she needed to know.

'I give you my word. I can meet you anywhere, Gloria. I have my own car now.' Mouse gave her the paper with her office number and the number in the block.

'Don't you get it? He has a few mates who have wives. If any of those spiteful bitches see me outside and it gets back to him and I get battered. To teach me a lesson…'

'But you…'

'I'll phone you, Mouse. Now go before someone sees you. He might be home early today coz it's a holiday.'

She left and hurried back to her car with her head down, already planning Gloria's escape.

*****

Mouse kept her word and didn't mention Gloria's situation to anyone. She did a bit of digging at the office. Gloria could declare her passport lost and they could get her another, legitimately. She toyed with the idea of a false compassionate case but that was a step too far. There was no way Mouse wanted to be bust to private again. Spike knew Mouse well enough to know that something was going on, but Mouse managed to convince her that she was out of sorts through worrying about Guy. Spike was a good mate, so let it go, hoping her friend would tell her in her own time.

The call came on the Monday afternoon. KC allowed Gloria to shop at the local NAAFI shop, less than three minutes walk away. After shopping, instead of using the British phone box in the married quarter area and risk being seen, she walked quickly to the German public phone, outside the *Westend Bar,* and called Mouse from there. There were few people who actually cared about Gloria's comings and goings, but KC had done such a good job on her that she was paranoid every time she left the flat.

'He's on duty tomorrow night. Can you come when it's dark and pick me up from the railway station on the main road?'

Mouse didn't know that Wickrath had a station, so Gloria gave her precise directions.

'We'll go to Schloss Wickrath. There won't be many there at night and there's plenty of shelter if it rains.' The Schloss was a parked area with an impressive castle, lake and greens. It was popular during the day when the weather was good, or in the summer evenings when bands were playing.

'OK. I'll be there. Is there a photo booth anywhere near you?'

Gloria explained that there was one outside the NAAFI Shop and Community Centre.

'You're going to need two passport photos. Can you get them before we meet?'

She agreed and they hung up.

Mouse went into work the following day as usual. The first thing she did was to put a blank passport application form in her bag.

It was already dark when she picked Gloria up as agreed. She felt like some sort of Eastern European spy as the girl from basic training pulled the car door closed behind her. Mouse half expected to hear a password but reined in her imagination to listen carefully to the directions. It wasn't far and they arrived at the Schloss car park a few minutes later. It was packed. She gave Gloria an enquiring look and the other woman shrugged her shoulders.

The air was still and humid as they entered the grounds. Mouse looked around. The imposing grey building was lit up like a Christmas tree even though it was the middle of summer, and a temporary bandstand had been erected opposite. People were heading towards the bandstand where the band was playing. They can watch the band, listen to the music and see the castle. Not a bad way to spend a summer evening thought Mouse.

'Shit. I didn't know this was on tonight,' said Gloria. Hearing the panic in her voice, Mouse tried to placate her.

'Are you likely to know anyone here?' The formal style of dress told Mouse instantly that this was primarily a German audience. There were a few people dressed in casual clothing, but the way they integrated into the crowd told her that they were locals.

'You're having a laugh aren't you? We're hardly likely to have any culture vultures living where I live.' She relaxed a little.

'It's actually easier to hide amongst a crowd of people, Gloria.'

'Come on, let's find somewhere more secluded.' Gloria's jaw set in a determined line and Mouse followed her as they moved further away from the castle, along the path into the green area. Stylish old-fashioned streetlights lit the way as they walked for a few minutes. They passed some people coming in the opposite direction and smiled back at the *Guten Abend* greetings. At a bend before coming to the lake, Gloria pointed to a covered shelter.

'You can't see it from here but there's a bench inside that shelter.'

'Looks ideal,' said Mouse as she followed her.

They sat down and Mouse extricated the paperwork from the plastic wallet. 'First things first. Passport application form.' She handed it to Gloria.

'Can you fill it in for me please. I'm rubbish with forms.'

'Nope. This application will come through my department and they all know my handwriting. I'll guide you through it though.'

It took fifteen tedious minutes for the form to be completed. Gloria worked herself up into a panic as they finished. 'What if he catches me?'

'He can only catch you if you tell him what you're doing. Have you lied to him before?'

'Yes, loads of times.'

'Did he know?'

'Most of the time, no. But never about anything as big as this.' Her eyes opened wide and looked like big saucers. Mouse thought she looked terrified.

'The bottom-line is do you want to get away?'

Gloria nodded.

'Do you want to go to someone for help. Maybe someone in the chain of command or perhaps a WRVS lady?'

This time she shook her head. 'If I did that he'd have to find out. Never mind what anybody says, he would be determined to come after me and to teach me a lesson. I know him well enough to know that.'

From recent experience Mouse knew she was absolutely right.

'Your options are limited, so it's up to you. Do you want my help or not?'

Gloria took some time to think while Mouse waited patiently.

'Why are you doing this?'

'Doing what? I'm not exactly risking my career am I?'

She studied her and Mouse started to feel uncomfortable under her gaze. 'I know there's more to it, Mouse. If we're going to trust each other, both of us need to be honest.'

'You know I left him at the altar. Yes?'

'He didn't tell me and it's not something he talks about, but yes, I do know that.'

'He was unfaithful and I should have finished it earlier, but I convinced myself I still loved him. It was only when I saw him in the church that I realised there was nothing there.'

'So?'

'So. It could have been me in your situation. And if it was, I'd like to think that somebody would help me.'

'Fair enough, but…'

'There's more.' She told Gloria about the attack in the accommodation block. 'I was convinced it was him. I didn't tell the military police because there weren't any witnesses and I didn't see his face. When I did a bit of digging I found out he wasn't due to be posted to Ayrshire Barracks until the following week. I just knew he'd have an alibi.'

'He did.' She looked down. 'He told me he'd had some business to attend to and if anyone asked, I was to say he was with me.'

'Didn't you wonder…'

'Of course. But I've learned not to ask too many questions. So as well as helping me, you'll get your revenge on him. Kill two birds so to speak.'

'Yup.'

Gloria's mouth twitched and Mouse tried unsuccessfully to suppress a giggle. They erupted into fits of laughter. When they calmed down, Gloria looked as if her laughter would turn to tears.

'How the fuck did I let myself get into this situation, Mouse? What happened to the young girl full of dreams of a career and independence?'

'Now you listen to me.' She held both her hands looking into her eyes as she did so. 'You're what? Twenty two, twenty three?'

'Twenty three, yes.'

'Your life isn't over. You're young enough to make a fresh start. Let's get you away from him first then you can resume the life that you want, on your own terms.'

Gloria smiled and for the first time in months, she had hope that she might actually be able to escape from her living nightmare.

'If you pull this off, I'll be forever in your debt.'

'If *we* pull this off, Gloria. It's going to take us both.'

Gloria pulled Mouse into her arms and hugged her tightly. Feeling a bit awkward after they broke apart, Mouse advised the next phase of the escape plan, Operation Vengeance as she called it, was to wait until the new passport arrived. She had no intention of giving Gloria any further details and told her she was working on it when Gloria asked what would follow. What she didn't know couldn't accidentally slip out when she was talking to, or being tormented by her prick of a husband.

*****

'Morning, sir. Can you sign... sorry.' Mouse hadn't noticed the boss was on the phone. He carried on talking but looked up and beckoned her into the office. She smiled. Even better.

'Can you sign these, please?' She mouthed as she put the papers on his desk. He trusted her and signed where indicated as she held the paper steady. Mouse assumed he hadn't looked at what he'd signed. So far, so good. She'd dismissed the idea of getting transport to take the application to the Consulate in Dusseldorf. That would definitely be taking the mickey and could also draw unneeded attention. She put it in the normal post. It would get there the following day anyway, and should only take a few weeks. That would give her enough time to make the other arrangements. Mouse was beginning to enjoy herself.

She arranged to visit Gloria's flat when there was no chance of KC being about.

'Nice three piece suite.' She ran her hand along the back of the burgundy leather sofa. She didn't know much about furniture but, like most women, recognised quality. This looked more expensive than a lance corporal could afford.

'I know. I love it,' said Gloria. 'He doesn't tell me about the money stuff but he had to sign an agreement in the shop and I heard three years being mentioned. The same with that.' She pointed to the state of the art stacked stereo system.

Mouse didn't know how any woman could be in a marriage where she had no idea of the couple's finances, in this day and age. Not for the first time she wondered why women would put up with what they did.

Fair play to Gloria, she kept a lovely home and it looked as if most of the furniture was their own, rather than the issue Army kit. She mentioned this as she walked around every room taking an inventory of each item.

'He would be embarrassed if his mates thought he couldn't afford something. So all this,' Gloria swept her arm around, 'isn't for my benefit. It's to save face.'

Mouse put down her pen and paper and smiled, rubbing her palms together. 'But in the long run Gloria, it will be for your benefit. Now we have work to do.'

They discussed each item and estimated the individual cost.

'KC's going on exercise the week after next by the way, for three weeks.'

Mouse nodded. 'Excellent. Your passport will be back by then so that's when you'll return to the UK. Have you told any of your family yet?'

Gloria explained that she hadn't yet plucked up the courage. 'You know my brother can't stand him and refused to speak to me. Well, I'm going to try him first. If I can get a job and ask David if I can stay with him and his wife for a while, KC might just leave me alone.'

'How come?'

'David's a Royal Marine. He's a fit bloke and knows a lot of other fit blokes.'

'Royal Marine? I take it he's, err, a bit taller than you?' Gloria was tiny and had been the smallest girl in basic training. Some of the others had wondered how she'd been accepted into the Army, but she'd just met the minimum height standard.

Gloria gave her a look and changed the subject. 'Fancy a cuppa?'

'Do we have time?' She nodded and they went to the kitchen.

Mouse went for a look out of the window, while Gloria boiled the kettle. It looked like it was still raining, but lightly.

'Shit, shit, shit. Quick!'

Gloria ran to the window and saw the two soldiers walking along the path. One lit a cigarette. Mouse didn't watch to see what they would do next. She had to get down stairs and out of the building before KC opened the door.

'Umbrella. Do you have one?'

She tried not to sound too frightened as the colour had already drained from Gloria's face. She looked like she'd been glued to the spot.

'Gloria. Move. Now.'

Gloria ran to the bedroom and brought out an umbrella. Mouse put her jacket on and did a rapid final check to ensure she hadn't left anything. She tucked her folder up under her jacket.

'Call me to let me know you're OK.'

'Will do.' Her voice shook.

'Act normal, and don't tell him anything. We're nearly there.'

Mouse left, closing the door gently behind her. Looking over the balcony she could see to the ground floor. Nobody was there. She ran down the stairs as fast as she could, then took a deep breath to compose herself. *Please don't let him be right outside.* Pulling her hood over her head to disguise as much of her face as she could, she opened the door. There was nobody there so they must still be talking. She put up the umbrella and angled it slightly to the side where she would pass them, but not at such an angle to draw too much attention to herself. She hurried along the path. The rain had stopped but she kept the umbrella up. She passed KC and his mate and hurried on.

'Oi!' KC shouted.

Mouse continued walking.

'Oi. It's stopped raining, you stupid cow.'

Mouse gave them the finger without turning around and carried on walking, umbrella up. She heard the men laughing behind her. Their laughter faded into the distance as she approached the end of the path. She risked a quick glance behind as she folded down the umbrella. They were still talking so she headed towards the NAAFI shop. Instead of going in she walked around to the back of the building and peeked around the corner. The soldiers went their separate ways. She waited until KC had entered his building then doubled back to the car park. Driving like a taxi driver having a sugar rush, Mouse left the Wickrath Estate as quickly as she could. Satisfied that she wasn't being followed, she pulled over a minute later to calm herself before resuming her journey. That had been too close for comfort and she hoped that Gloria was OK.

*****

Gloria wasn't OK. He'd asked if she'd seen anyone, she told him she hadn't and he'd decided not to believe her. She took the beating silently, as she usually did. He'd wanted to have sex with her afterwards but she'd refused.

'Want another beating then, do you?' KC thrust his head forward but Gloria didn't even flinch.

'Do what you must, but you're not having my body. Unless of course you take it and that would make you a rapist.'

He reeled back. Rape her? What sort of man did she think he was?

'I'm going for a pint.' He slammed the door and Gloria smiled grimly to herself at the small victory as she tried to put the pain to the back of her mind. There was light at the end of the tunnel after all.

Chapter 8

The Sixth Sense newspaper was the publication for British Forces in Germany. Much like a UK town newspaper, the weekly carried local stories, sports news, advertisements and details of what was happening in the community. If necessary, it was also used to inform of changes in policy or anything else considered important by the chain of command. Immature soldiers sometimes used the paper for joke advertisements such as putting their mates' branded football team gear up for sale when the teams they supported were performing poorly. This caused hilarity amongst all except the poor sod who was the butt of the joke. Mouse didn't usually read the paper, but decided that she needed to look at a few issues so she could write the best adverts possible to sell Gloria's belongings. She didn't want to think of them as KC's.

This part of Op Vengeance wouldn't be easy to implement, but with a little luck...

Mouse went to have a word with Frau Mueller. She often chatted to the older woman who was in an office on her own. Frau Mueller enjoyed telling her young Welsh friend all about her family and the competitions into which she'd entered her Boxer dog, Fritz. Sworn to secrecy, she agreed that Mouse could use her telephone extension for the purpose requested and Mouse mentally ticked another box on her to do list.

Mouse or Danny Roper, the corporal in the office, usually collected the mail from the post room. They distributed it within the branch then dealt with anything for their main office. She made a cuppa and told her colleagues that she'd do a food run to the NAAFI cafe within the HQ, and collect the mail on the way back.

'Who are you trying to impress?'

'Nobody, Danny. I just need to stretch my legs.'

On her return she dished out the rolls they'd ordered and put hers to one side. While they were all busy with their tea and rolls, Mouse quickly separated the mail and distributed it. The package from the consulate had arrived so she opened it. Inside were separate envelopes addressed to units throughout the British Army of the Rhine. She felt the one addressed to Rhine Area Workshop. Good, there was only one passport inside. She put the envelope into her handbag. Nobody would call to ask about it because they didn't know she'd applied for a new passport for one of their dependants. She went to the post tray and took the *Special Delivery Register.* The envelopes containing passports for other personnel would have to be signed for, so she spent the next few minutes recording the details in the register and stamping up the envelopes. Danny offered to take them to the Post Room so Mouse let him get on with it. She couldn't wait to get back to her room to check that all was in order with Gloria's passport.

As soon as the HQ NAAFI Shop opened on Thursday of the following week, Mouse made an excuse to leave the office and rushed out to buy *The Sixth Sense.* The phones were quiet for a change, and Danny and Staff Wilson were out doing their Basic Fitness Test and wouldn't be back just yet. Members of the Women's Royal Army Corps had to do a separate test, and Mouse was due to do hers the following week.

She opened the paper at the adverts pages and quickly scanned down to find those that she had placed. Great, they were all there. She had listed all of Gloria's belongings as agreed, but under two different names and phone numbers so that if KC happened to get hold of the paper while he was on exercise, he would hopefully take no notice. The phone numbers to ring were her office and Frau Mueller's. She'd asked callers to ring at lunchtime when everyone else would be out, so that wouldn't be a problem.

Carried away with the planning for Op Vengeance, Mouse hadn't figured that just because the adverts said to call at lunchtime, people would do. Not everybody was in the Army, and even those that were, were keen to purchase bargains before anyone else got their hands on them.

'It's for you, again,' Danny handed her the receiver for the third time. 'Tell these bloody people to call back in your own time. We're supposed to be doing an important job here, Mouse. It's not *Sale of the Century* you know.' He obviously thought he was funny.

She gave him an apologetic smile. He needed to work on his one liners but now wasn't the time.

'That's right, burgundy. It's only eight months old. I can show you a photo but you're the third person who's called to say they're interested.'

Danny watched, frowning. Mouse turned away from him and spoke quietly into the phone.

'Not lunchtime, sorry. I can meet you outside the main NAAFI after work. OK, see you there.' She scribbled something onto her notepad and hung up.

'Right. I know you're up to something. What's going on.'

'It's nothing to do with work, nothing illegal, and none of your business, so...'

'Call for you, Mouse. In my office.'

Frau Mueller interrupted so she rushed out of the office and left Danny even more curious.

Later that day Major Best decided to stay in for lunch, which was unheard of, and Mouse didn't have a Plan B. Nobody else was about. She'd answered a few enquiries about Gloria's possessions, and one work query. About to tuck into her sandwich, the boss walked into the office and sat down at Danny's desk. He placed The Sixth Sense on the desk and opened it at the adverts page.

'So, Corporal Warbutton. Does this have anything to do with the passport application you asked me to sign?'

Mouse couldn't hide her surprise.

'Close your mouth, girl. You look like a startled trout.'

Charming. Was her first thought, quickly followed by panic over what to reveal.

'I'm waiting.'

She'd seen Major Best when he was absolutely furious, fortunately he didn't look like that at the moment. He sat back in Danny's chair and folded his arms, his patience clearly nearing its limit. She knew he could smell bullshit at a hundred paces. She wasn't going to credit him with a lack of intelligence, as Staff Sergeant Farrow used to.

'Yes, sir. It does.' Mouse began her explanation, but stopped when the boss interrupted.

'So how do you know this woman and her husband?'

'I was in the same platoon as Gloria in basic training. I didn't even know she was out of the Army. I was engaged to her husband a while back. He's the one who attacked me in the accommodation block but I couldn't prove it. It would have been worse if I'd accused him without any evidence, so I decided to keep quiet.'

'And convince his wife to leave him?'

'I thought you knew me better than that, sir.'

Suitably berated, Major Best asked her to continue.

'I wanted to get my own back on KC, but wasn't sure what to do. So I found out that he was married and where they live.'

He nodded encouragement.

'It's Wickrath actually. Anyway, sir. I discovered that he abuses his wife and wondered if I could help...'

'Whoa. How the hell did you find out about that?'

She explained and added how surprised she was when she discovered she actually knew his wife. 'Gloria refuses point blank to seek help. She's a victim, sir but if anyone reports *him,* she won't admit to it and her life will be even worse. I'm offering her a way out.'

'And getting your revenge into the bargain?'

'That's a bonus, sir. I've called it Operation Vengeance.' She laughed until she saw his grave expression then carried on. 'As far as I'm aware I haven't done anything illegal, but I know I've been devious.'

He gave her a look.

'Except saying the passport was lost of course. I'm sorry if I've betrayed your trust and all I ask is that you do nothing until Gloria has escaped. I'll take it on the chin then, however you decide to punish me.'

Major Best didn't know whether to give her a bollocking or a pat on the back. She was definitely the sort of friend to have in a crisis, but that didn't mean he could condone her behaviour. He needed time to think and she deserved to sweat for a bit.

'You've told me everything I need to know.'

'What are you going to do, sir?'

'That's for me to know and you to find out, Corporal Warbutton. And you will find out precisely what's going to happen tomorrow morning. Be in the office at seven fifteen.'

'Yes, sir.'

She had to somehow get through the rest of the day and night before discovering what her future held, and Gloria's for that matter. Mouse decided to carry on as if the Op was going ahead. There was no point in telling Gloria and have her worrying about something she had no control over.

Chapter 9

Elaine now knew that filing details of the suicide note and Guy's reaction into the deepest recesses of her brain would not allow her to get on with her life as normally as she had hoped it would. It was like a festering wound that just wouldn't go away. Her girlfriend Jill had noticed the change in her and was worried that it was something to do with their relationship. The sooner it was out in the open, the better. They could all get on with their lives then and she would apply for special duties, whatever Guy Halfpenny decided to do. Elaine planned to tell Jill during their week in Spain, and hoped she wouldn't ruin the entire holiday for her.

It was the beginning of September and the air was balmy as they walked along the strip towards their favourite beach cocktail bar. Even far away from anyone who might know them, they rarely held hands or made public displays of affection – the world wasn't ready for this. Leaning against the bar with a Tequila Sunrise in hand, they watched the glorious sunset in silence. The sun looked massive as it dipped further down the horizon, painting the sky in stunning pink and orange hues as it did so.

'You look lovely tonight.' Jill broke the silence and Elaine smiled and took one of her hands without a second thought about what others might think.

'So. Is this where you tell me it's been great but you're dumping me?' asked Jill.

'Is that what you think? Really?' Elaine dropped her hand.

'All I know is that something's been bugging you for ages. It's as if you're somewhere else. Every time I try to talk to you, you change the subject. What am I supposed to think?'

Elaine closed her eyes. Here goes. 'I wanted to kill myself.'

'What the...'

'All that business with Mouse and I thought you wanted to finish with me. It was a moment of madness and then the crash...'

'You caused the crash?'

'No. Not at all. But I went out with the intention of doing so. I wasn't myself, Jill,' she grabbed both of her hands. 'I was distraught and didn't know what I was doing. So now you know what a coward I am, you'd be better off without me.'

Jill was quiet while she took it in and Elaine held her breath. 'If I was going to leave you it would be for not telling me, not for threatening to do something in a moment of madness, then changing your mind. Come here you stupid bugger.' Elaine walked to her lover and they hugged, oblivious to the few people around them until the barman coughed. Laughing nervously, Elaine returned to her barstool.

'So you've been stressing about not telling me and hiding it from Mouse too, and Grace?'

Elaine nodded.

'Nobody knows then?'

'Not exactly.' She explained that Guy had found her note and the consequences of the find.

'So he's been blackmailing you?'

'Well not exactly...'

'Yes, Elaine. That's exactly what it is, blackmail. Emotional blackmail. Wait until I see that bastard I'll give him a piece of my mind and some.'

'It's over, Jill. When I go to Germany to see Mouse and Grace I'll tell them both. I'll also tell Mouse about Guy's involvement. I know her, she'll be bloody furious too. Firstly, because I didn't tell her, then because he didn't tell her and also about the blackmail. The good thing, if you can call it that, is she'll be more annoyed with him than she is with me.' She gave an ironic chuckle. Jill wasn't so sure and for once in her life, managed to do the right thing by keeping her mouth shut. Finishing their cocktails, they paid the bill and went to find a suitable restaurant for their evening meal. Jill was relieved but felt different. Something had changed. Elaine was the strong one in their relationship and had always looked after her. Now Jill realised that Elaine was the one who needed to be protected. She made a silent vow that she would be the one to look after her. Forever.

*****

'Lance Corporal Warbutton. In my office, now.' He normally called her Corporal Warbutton and there was usually kindness in his tone. Not this morning, even though nobody else was about yet. It didn't bode well.

'Yes, sir.' She walked into his office, not bothering to ask if he would like a coffee. She didn't take a seat; thinking it more appropriate to wait and see if he asked.

'Sit down.'

It couldn't be that bad then. As Major Best was sitting at his small conference table, rather than at his desk, she took the chair at the table opposite him.

'Good morning, sir.'

'Good morning. I'll cut straight to the chase.' He leaned back and folded his arms. 'I'm annoyed and impressed...'

'I'm sorry, sir. I know it was wrong...' She stopped mid flow. *Had he just said he was impressed?* 'Did I hear you right there, Major Best?'

'You certainly did. I am very annoyed at your deviousness, but impressed at your initiative and determination to help a friend in need, despite the fact that your original intention was to exact revenge on your ex.'

'Thank you, sir. I think. Does that mean I'm not in the...'

'Not at all. You are still in it. Right up to your neck Corporal Warbutton.'

That was slightly better. Good.

'Do you want to stay in G1 Division and in this branch, or perhaps go and work down at 29 Company?'

He appeared to have a twinkle in his eye like he was enjoying himself. The swine! Was he really going to move her?

'No, sir. I want to stay here.'

'Hmm.' Major Best leaned forward and looked into her eyes. Mouse looked away first. 'Can I trust you not to do anything like this again?'

'Yes...'

'Think very carefully, Corporal Warbutton, before you answer that question.

'I have, sir. I've learnt my lesson. And if I can be frank?'

'Go ahead.'

'Well. Once this is done Gloria will be safe and I will have paid back KC. As much as I'm able to,' she gave a wry smile. Searching her conscience Mouse had to admit that she would like to see KC physically damaged. She knew that made her a bad person, but couldn't help it. He was going to be humiliated so perhaps that would be as bad. 'There'll be no need to do anything like this again.'

'But what about when you meet the next victim who needs saving and she asks for help?'

'Gloria didn't actually ask for my help, sir. I convinced her to go ahead with this. I promise that I'll keep my head down and stay out of trouble. I am genuinely sorry, but only for...'

'Quit while you're ahead.'

'Yes, sir.' Mouse waited. There was something else to come, she could sense it.

'I really should report it to Lance Corporal Cooke's chain of command, then the attack can be properly investigated too.' Major Best was looking at his hands while drumming his fingers on his desk and had spoken more to himself, she thought. Mouse silently willed him to change his mind. He made her sweat for a few more seconds before speaking.

'You can stay here and this won't go any further on one condition.'

'Anything.'

'I'm going to need your assistance with an ongoing investigation. That's all I can tell you today, but you may be required to answer some questions...'

'Staff Sergeant Wilson?'

'Pardon?'

'I knew he was up to something.'

Major Best gave nothing away but Mouse was on a roll.

'He whispers on the phone then hangs up abruptly when someone goes in the office. And he has that leery look about him that gives most women the creeps. There's rumours too, about his wife. She's with the Signals up country isn't she? I'm right aren't I, sir?' She judged that it wasn't the time or the place to tell her boss about the incident in Aldershot. Not just yet.

'Let's leave it at that for now. Do I need to remind you that this discussion is only between the two of us?'

'Understood, sir. It won't go any further.' She left the office and meant exactly what she'd said. She needed to concentrate on getting Gloria out of the country the following week, and would then try to discover what Staff Sergeant Wilson was up to. Hopefully all of that and looking forward to seeing her best mates would be enough to take her mind off Guy, for at least some of the time.

Chapter 10

After the surrender by the Argentinians, it was decided that the marines and paras were to be kept on the outskirts of Port Stanley. This decision was made in order to avoid any potential reaction from the Argentines if the British troops were moved into the town too soon.

Apart from the major general's surrender party, the military police were the only British soldiers there for a while. Looking at the others, Guy could see that it was weird for all of them. Captain Mac, the RMP OC, had told them he'd received orders from the major general to disarm and search the Argies. On top of that, all the information had to be documented. The marines and paras arrived a while later when the bosses judged that the enemy were unlikely to do anything stupid. They helped to line up the Argies in groups of two hundred. Captain Mac didn't mind mucking in and getting his hands dirty with the rest of them. It was just as well as there were only eighteen military police and thousands of fully armed Argentinians. Guy could see the excitement in the eyes of some of the enemy. The RMPs started work. As Guy searched one man, the prisoner started shouting something in Spanish and waving his arms.

'What the fuck?' The owner of the voice appeared at his side and secured the man's arms behind his back. They found bullets in the breeches of his gun and a primed grenade in his belt. A look passed between Guy and the marine who'd come to assist. It wasn't over yet. If one of the prisoners wanted to meet his maker, he could do so and take out a whole lot of the British force while he was at it. They were all tense now, knowing that anything could happen. Thankfully, it didn't. Following the disarming, all the prisoners had to be documented. There was a dire shortage of paper so they had to improvise, even writing on the back of cigarette packets in a few cases. The hoard of possessions was stacked and Guy sighed to himself. It had taken a week to disarm, document and get them all properly organized. Now they had to check with the locals to see if any of the items belonged to them. For some bizarre reason there were hundreds of torches; he was too tired to wonder why.

To a man they were all exhausted, physically and mentally. Guy crawled into his sleeping bag and was asleep within seconds. *He twitched as the bomb hit the boat. He was sitting on the grass with some of the other military policemen. It seemed surreal as they watched from their safe spot ashore as the boat burst into flames and fellow soldiers flew into the air. Inexplicably, Larry his close friend who'd died in Germany was on board. His body landed and his limbs were deformed and sticking out at all different angles. Then Guy was on the boat with them. Instead of trying to help those that could be helped, he walked around the deck, just watching, unaffected by the chaos and the flames. Someone tapped him on the shoulder. He turned and the man that faced him was on fire, the flames burning the skin from his face. He laughed until his eyes popped out.*

'For fuck's sake, Halfpenny. Shut up!'

He lay still for a moment, disorientated, until he remembered where he was. 'OK. Sorry.' But the man who had shouted was already out of it. Snoring loudly. Guy was knackered. It was pitch black so must still be stupid o'clock. He didn't want to go straight back to sleep in case the nightmare returned, so got up as quietly as he could and went outside. It was well below freezing and he stayed outside until all remnants of the nightmare had left him. Once they had, Guy got back into his sleeping bag and closed his eyes. This time he slept without interruption.

*****

Despite what she'd said to Jill, Elaine wanted to inform Grace about the note before they all met up for the weekend in Germany. It wasn't an easy letter to write but it was cathartic. Once Elaine had posted it she felt as if a load had been lifted. She knew her friend would contact her as soon as she received the letter. Two weeks later she wondered if all was well with Grace. Perhaps she couldn't forgive her for what she'd done? Perhaps the letter had been lost in the post? Perhaps, perhaps.

Grace phoned the following day.

'Sorry I didn't call earlier.'

Elaine waited but all she said was that Graham had been warned for a tour in the Falklands.

'When's he off?'

'We don't know. Usual Army stuff. I suppose they'll make them hurry up and wait, then everything will be last minute.'

She chuckled as Grace had expected. There was silence for a few seconds.

'Sorry about telling you in a letter, but I needed you to know before I speak to Mouse.'

'Why?'

It threw her. 'Well, you know. I...'

'You promised no more secrets, Elaine, and you've broken that promise already.'

'But.'

'But what?'

It wasn't like Grace to be so unforgiving so Elaine was taken aback. Still, none of them were the people they were when they'd met at Guildford. Even so, she couldn't fathom what might have happened to her to make her quite so unsympathetic.

'Look I'm sorry. I've got a bad feeling about Graham going away and it's making me...'

'No, I'm sorry. That's fine. Graham will be OK you know. The war's over and they're starting to send the Argy POWs home. They should all be gone within the next month or so.'

'I can't explain it, Elaine. It's just a feeling I've got. Anyway, there's no point worrying about that when he hasn't even left yet. What about you? Are you all right now?'

'Yup.'

'I mean you're absolutely sure that you're not going to do anything like that again?'

'Yes, absolutely. I'm not looking forward to telling Mouse about the letter and what Guy's doing. I have to do it though because, like you said, I promised.'

'A promise is a promise.'

She sounded harsh again and Elaine had had enough. 'Grace. I haven't actually broken that promise. I just haven't told you both yet. I wanted to be sure that I was all right and that by telling Mouse, I'm making the right decision.'

'OK. But you should have done it earlier.' Her criticism was met with silence so she continued. 'I assume that you wrote to me because you want my opinion?' she didn't wait for an answer. 'Well my opinion is that you should have told us both before now. We're friends and we're supposed to help each other out, no matter where the Army decides to send us.'

'Ah, right.' It was like being caught out lying to your parents as a youngster, and Elaine felt like shit.

'I'm sorry, Grace. Really sorry.' She resisted the urge to say it wouldn't happen again.

'You'll have to tell her at the start of the weekend, whether it puts the mockers on it or not. You know that don't you?'

'Yeah, I will.'

They discussed some less emotional subjects before saying goodbye.

'See you in a few weeks,' said Elaine.

'Will do. I'm looking forward to us three being together again, whatever happens.'

*****

It was Tuesday evening and Mouse was on her way to Gloria's flat. They'd struck lucky. She'd arranged to meet one of the buyers there. The couple were newly married and newly posted in to Krefeld, which meant that he was probably in a different Corps and lived far enough away not to know KC or any of his mates. The wife was also new to the Army way of life and was mortified to discover the uncomfortable two-seater sofa with bright orange covers when they moved into their first married quarter. Insisting on having her own belongings, her husband had scoured the adverts in *The Sixth Sense* and arranged to buy a number of items through Mouse.

Gloria looked distracted as she attempted to show them around. Mouse gave her a look and she mouthed that she'd explain later. She wasn't doing the best job of selling her stuff, so Mouse took over.

'The suite's beautiful isn't it? Top of the range you know.'

The woman nodded. It was obvious that she wanted it but they wondered if it were too expensive for her husband's pocket.

'OK, we'll do you a deal. Fifty Marks off if you buy the bed as well. That's our final offer, take it or leave it.'

He stroked his chin contemplating the price. 'It's still a bit pricey. We'll have a think about it and let you know. What's your phone number, love?' He ignored Mouse and asked Gloria.

Gloria hesitated and Mouse answered for her. 'I'm sorry but one of the reasons this is such a good deal is because Gloria wants a quick sale,' she walked to the door. 'Thanks for coming. I'm sorry you've had a wasted journey.'

The man made to walk out but his wife nudged him. 'Can you give us a few minutes please? We're not going anywhere just yet.'

'Certainly,' said Mouse as she ushered Gloria into the kitchen.

Hearing the woman talking quietly, Mouse figured they'd got the sale they wanted. There was a little more leeway but not too much; Gloria would need some money to live on until she found a job in Cornwall.

'What's wrong with you tonight,' she whispered.

'I phoned my brother. He was very frosty at first.' She looked like she was about to cry so Mouse put a hand on her arm.

'Are you sure you want to talk about this now?'

Gloria took a deep breath and nodded. 'He's been trying to get hold of me for ages. He's written loads of letters, which have all been returned unopened. My family think I want nothing to do with them because they don't approve of KC.'

She shook her head and explained that she'd told him the truth. 'He wants to come over here and rip KC's head off and shit down his throat.'

'I take it he's not happy then?' Mouse smirked and Gloria laughed.

'You could say that. Anyway, I'm going to stay with them on Thursday night and he's sure his wife won't have a problem with that. I hardly know her but if he says it'll be OK, I'm sure it will. My mother's ill so I don't want to go home and risk a visit from KC.'

'But we both know that KC's not likely to have a go at you if that means the risk of a good kicking, or worse, from a Royal Marine and some of his mates?'

'Exactly.'

'Why didn't you call David earlier?'

Gloria folded her arms and looked down, unable or refusing to make eye contact with Mouse. 'You don't know what it's like when someone wears you down, Mouse. It seems like he's constantly telling me how ugly and useless I am. How I'm lucky to have him and if I wasn't so bloody useless, he wouldn't have to hit me,' she shuddered. 'He only does it to teach me a lesson.'

'We're ready to do a deal.' The woman popped her head around the kitchen door and smiled, it was laced with sympathy. Gloria pulled herself together and smiled back.

'We're happy with nine hundred Marks for the suite...'

'But...' she silenced her husband with a look.

'As I said, nine hundred is a fair price. Come on, Paul, before she changes her mind.' The deal was done and Paul ran down the stairs to get his mate who would help to load the furniture onto the truck he'd borrowed. The money exchanged hands.

'Good luck, love, I hope everything works out for you.'

Gloria thanked the woman who left shortly after.

There were two more visitors that evening and one due the following day. If all went to plan the flat would be empty by Thursday. As Gloria said goodbye to Mouse at the door, her neighbour's door opened.

'Lots of comings and goings at your place tonight.'

Hello Gloria, how are you keeping? would have been nice, but no chance thought Gloria. 'I'm very well thanks. How are you?' she was feeling mischievous and both girls giggled.

The neighbour looked confused which made it even funnier. 'Well?'

'Yeah. Don't tell anyone, but KC's fallen behind with the payments so the good stuff's had to go.'

'Ooh. Don't worry, you're secret's safe with me.' She closed her door to the sound of the younger women's laughter. She didn't understand what was so funny. Why would someone be so happy about selling all of their belongings? She had no idea but wondered if Pat might. She'd give her a call to see what she thought of it all.

Two days later Gloria looked around her empty flat and smiled. Her two bags and what she had in her purse were all that was left from her short marriage. The bruises from the last beating had faded and Gloria hoped that, with time, the memories would too. Mouse had been true to her word and everything was gone. Items that hadn't been sold within the three-day period that they'd allotted had been given away. It had been impossible to keep it quiet and as Gloria thought about what would happen if word got to KC, her expression changed from happy to haunted. *Come on Mouse, hurry up.* She had no reason to doubt her friend; she'd been as good as her word as far as Op Vengeance was concerned. From the advice about squirrelling away as many Deutschmarks as she could from her housekeeping, to obtaining her new passport, advertising and selling her belongings, and booking her flight through the travel agent on camp. Mouse had also put her in touch with Army Legal Aid and KC would discover a letter from the lawyer, on his return from exercise. Gloria giggled nervously as she imagined his reaction when he read the letter telling him that she was divorcing him. He would be liable for all outstanding hire purchase agreements, which would make him even more furious, and the married quarter monthly rent until he moved back into the single soldier accommodation. But the bottom line was that she would be free. She could move on with her life and put her disastrous marriage behind her. COME ON MOUSE! The doorbell rang and Gloria had a bad feeling. *Please God, don't let him find out until I'm with my brother*. She opened the door tentatively, convinced her abusive husband had returned.

'All ready then?' Mouse was taken aback when Gloria threw herself into her arms.

Gloria chattered away on the journey to the airport, sounding like a flock of sparrows. Now she realised escape and the possibility of a new life was a reality, she couldn't suppress her excitement.

They hugged then said goodbye, before Gloria went through customs. 'I will never be able to thank you enough for this, Mouse. You are a true friend and I couldn't and wouldn't have done it without you.'

'Glad to be of assistance.' It was inadequate, but there were no words to express her happiness for Gloria and the satisfaction of getting her own back on KC. 'Write and let me know how you're getting on, but don't put your address on the letter. You know, just in case.'

'Got it.'

'If you need me, contact my brother at the address I gave you and let him know where I can find you.' It was likely that KC would go after her to start with and Mouse didn't want to be the one to give him Gloria's address, inadvertently or otherwise. They hugged again and said their final farewell. Gloria turned and gave Mouse one last wave before disappearing through the Customs channel.

*****

For the next few days, Mouse felt compelled to look behind her, everywhere she went. She knew without a shadow of a doubt that KC would pay her a visit, as soon as the shit hit the fan. Major Best said that he'd look out for her, but with the best will in the world he couldn't be with her twenty four seven. She knew KC would be charged if she were attacked again, but it was no comfort knowing that she might sustain physical injuries before he would be punished. She hadn't confided all her concerns to the boss and despite her worries, life settled down to the usual, albeit more tense routine. Elaine and Grace were due to visit at the weekend. She was taking leave on Friday and Monday and had their whole visit planned out. They were due to arrive on Thursday night and Mouse could hardly contain her excitement. That would be a week after Gloria had left so if KC decided to pay her a visit then, at least she'd have the company of her good friends to go up against him. Spike was also going to spend some time with them and she knew they'd all get on great.

Mouse had felt an atmosphere in work but had put it down to her nervousness about the KC situation. Major Best had asked her to pay particular attention to the calls made by and to Staff Sergeant Wilson and she took on the task like a true pro. Standing by the door she listened intently. He seemed to be discussing porn movies and some sort of payment, but Mouse wasn't sure. He looked up as she breezed into the office.

'Hi, staff,' She said, then pretended she'd only just noticed he was on the phone. 'Ooh, sorry. You're on the phone.'

He told the person he was talking to, to hold on, and covered the receiver with his hand. 'This is a delicated case, Corporal Warbutton. Give me a few minutes.'

'Yes, staff.' Mouse left the office, reported her findings to Major Best, then made her way to the German canteen. As she chomped on her delicious roll filled with just the right amount of ham and soft cheese, she congratulated herself on her performance, which she reckoned would have rivalled anything by Meryl Streep.

She'd planned on opening the letter from Guy in the privacy of her room that night, but the temptation was too much. She moved to a table further from the door and opened it.

Fifteen minutes later she was back in the office. He loved and missed her more than he thought possible. Mouse was elated at his offer of marriage. They'd already talked about it but it somehow seemed more real with the words written on the bluey. She'd suggest a long engagement, possibly years. The ache in her body was worse than being ill. This was much harder than when he was in the UK and she was in Germany. Anything could happen all those miles away but she was thankful that the war was over and most of the prisoners would soon be on their way back to Argentina, according to Guy that was. She wondered if it would be easier, knowing that very soon he would be back to his usual pre-war duties of dealing with errant squaddies.

Still no visit from KC and Thursday arrived without any further drama.

Chapter 11

KC was absolutely knackered. It had been a long three weeks and he stank to high heaven after spending most of it in the field. To be fair they all stank, but it wasn't until they returned to their unit and were around clean people, that they realised how bad they were. They all deserved the name of *Pongo,* the derogatory term for the Army used by the other Services. He picked up his mail, jumped into his car and made his way home as quickly as he could. Gloria hadn't answered the phone when he'd tried to call her from camp to let her know he'd be back a day early, and to give her instructions about tea and what he expected her to wear. He provided for the bloody woman and this was the way she thanked him. Frustrated, he knew he'd have to teach her another lesson. He'd get cleaned up and have some food first though.

There was no answer so KC dug out his keys. The nosey cow next door opened her door before he got into his flat. 'She's not there.'

He was too tired to put up with his interfering neighbour. 'Fuck off.' He opened the door and walked in. She walked back into her flat and smiled. The smug bastard was getting what he deserved.

As he looked around his eyes sent the message to his tired brain that his flat was empty. 'Gloria. GLOOORIAAA!' Instead of the smell of something delicious cooking as it should have been, all he could smell was bleach and ammonia. When it clicked, he went berserk. Nothing was happening on the patch that Wednesday night so, hearing the noise, the neighbour decided to call the military police. After all she smirked, she was only being a good citizen. He might be at risk of damaging himself as well as destroying the flat. She also called her best mate after hanging up. It didn't take long for word to go around. Despite his verbal and physical protestations, they decided he should stay at the station overnight, for his own good and to ensure he couldn't do any further damage to the flat; he'd already broken two windows and the bedroom door. He spat at the woman next door as she stood staring with arms folded.

'Get your fucking hands off me! It's that stupid bitch Gloria you should arrest.' Doors opened as other neighbours wanted to watch the action. The two military police, one male one female, had their work cut out restraining him when they walked him down the stairs, even though they'd cuffed him and his hands were behind his back. He was still putting up a fight and screaming at the injustice of his treatment. More curtains twitched when the police secured him in their car.

Later when he'd been processed none too gently, KC had calmed and had time to think. He knew without a doubt that Gloria wouldn't have acted on her own. She must have had help and encouragement, especially with obtaining a new passport. He was totally knackered but his last thought before sleeping on the urine-stained mattress in his cell, was that both his wife and ex fiancé would pay for this humiliation, and pay dearly. He had no doubt that Mouse was involved and he was going to make sure that she would regret it.

*****

Grace was driving from her unit in Celle and agreed to pick Elaine up from Dusseldorf Airport. Mouse wasn't expecting them until after six. She left the office at five, leaving herself plenty of time to shower and change so they could leave the camp if that's what the girls wanted. For security reasons, they weren't allowed to go off camp in uniform unless travelling to another base or were married personnel who travelled to work from their quarter – then they had to wear civilian jackets. It seemed like a strange rule to Mouse. British Forces cars were easily recognisable with their British Forces Germany number plates. The colours of some of the military cars were worse than the bright oranges and purples of the Army furniture covers; both made easy targets for the bloody IRA, who had a habit of occasionally hiding a bomb under one of the cars, just to keep them all on their toes. They'd all been issued with mirrors on long poles and shown the correct way to check under their vehicle. During security briefings, the instructions were always accompanied by a gruesome video of a soldier who had forgotten to check. He urged listeners not to end up like him as the camera panned from his face to the stumps where his legs should have been.

They'd had a few days of non-stop rain and walking towards the accommodation block, the field next to the Rheindahlen Rooms was bright and shiny; the grass well nourished by the wet summer weather. It was strange how she noticed nature more when she was in a good mood. Mouse turned the corner at the Rheindahlen Rooms and screamed when two people jumped out on her. Convinced that KC had come to get her, she made to sprint until her brain finally caught up with her limbs and she did a double take. They all laughed as her screaming was followed by group hugs.

'You're early. When did you get here? Are you booked in yet?' She looked around. 'Where's your car, Grace?'

'Yes. About an hour ago, yes and over there.' Elaine replied and the girls linked arms as they walked to Grace's yellow mini.

'That's a bit snazzy and soooooo you.' They laughed again and chattered away, trying to catch up with month's worth of news in a few minutes.

'What do you want to do tonight?'

'Shall we go somewhere quiet? We've got a lot of catching up to do. You can show us all the party places at the weekend,' said Grace.

Mouse noticed the look that passed between her two friends. She knew Elaine had something to tell her but decided not to say anything. Yet. She had no desire to put the dampers on their mood but whatever it was, it was obvious to Mouse that Grace already knew. She couldn't help thinking *here we go again.*

The Marley Club was always busy, but away from the main party room there was a back bar where soldiers could play pool, darts and have a drink and chat without having to shout over the sound of the music. It was a bit smoky at times but they could always sit outside if it was too much to bear. This was where Mouse decided to take her friends.

'Tell me you don't want to eat in the cookhouse?' Although it catered for military personnel of many nationalities, it wasn't most people's favourite place to eat. She didn't wait for their answer. 'We'll have a few bevvies, you can confess, Elaine, then if we're still speaking we'll get food from the Marley chippy.'

Elaine laughed nervously.

'Actually, Mouse. Can we have a chat in your room and go out later, if you still want to?'

Shit! 'That bad eh?' she chuckled. The silence answered her question and she frowned. They were quiet during the short car journey to the accommodation. Mouse keyed the code into the simplex lock on the outside door and her friends followed her inside.

'Make a brew while I go for a quick shower.'

Elaine and Grace looked at each other. This wasn't like their nosey friend. 'What have you done with the real Mouse?'

'Tee fucking hee he.' They all laughed and Grace received a playful punch from Mouse on her way out. Once she'd left Elaine answered Grace's look.

'It doesn't matter what I think, Grace. I made a promise so I have to tell her. She needs to know the truth.'

They made the coffees and waited. Mouse breezed into her room smelling of apple shampoo, looking as if she hadn't a care in the world. 'Spill, Elaine,' she said as she started to towel dry her hair.

'There's no easy way to say this so I'll just tell it how it is.'

Mouse took a pair of socks from a drawer, inspected them, returned them, removed another pair...

'Can you just stop that and pay attention?'

Suitably chastised, she sat on her bed with her arms folded. Elaine sighed. 'The day of my car accident I wanted to end my life...'

Mouse flew to her friend's side and put an arm around her.

'It's OK, Mouse. I didn't go through with it.'

'Obviously. But the accident...'

'Let me explain. I knew I'd let you down badly. Guy was pissed off with me and I thought Jill wouldn't want to know me any more. My world had imploded and I was feeling more than sorry for myself.' She looked at both of them. Grace smiled encouragingly but Elaine could see that Mouse was finding it difficult to keep quiet.

'My head was all over the place and I wrote a note, planning to end it all. I just wanted life to go away. It didn't take long for me to clear my head once I started driving. Something about watching the miles go by always makes me see things clearly and it wasn't long before I looked at the note and laughed at my self-pity. I made up my mind to get in touch with you to try to make amends, and also planned to tell Jill and ask her not to leave me. Until the car coming in the opposite direction was on my side of the road.'

'Are you OK now?'

'I'm fine. It was just a stupid couple of hours of self-pity which I've regretted ever since.'

'Thanks for being honest with me. I would have worried about you but I'd never think any less of you, Elaine. You know that don't you?'

'Me too,' said Grace.

'I do know that, thanks…'

'Right.' Now dressed in tight jeans and yellow t-shirt, Mouse brushed her damp hair and secured it in a ponytail with a red elastic tie. 'Shall we get going then?' She grabbed her leather jacket.

'That's not all.'

She sat down and waited.

'As you know Guy was the first on the scene after the accident. He found my note.'

'I don't think so, Elaine. He would have mentioned it.'

'I'm sorry, but he did find the note. I didn't realise straight away.'

'Then how…'

'I asked his advice about training for special duties in Northern Ireland. I know he did a bit of research...' she stopped and sighed deeply.

'Go on,' said Grace. Gently encouraging Elaine to continue. Mouse felt her heart race and knew she wasn't going to like what was coming.

'He doesn't think I'm suitable for special duties.'

'Because of the note?'

'Yes. No matter how much I told him I was fine, he didn't believe me,' she lowered her voice. 'He threatened to grass me up, Mouse, unless I agreed not to apply.'

'You cannot be serious.' *Did I really just say that?* wondered Mouse. Despite the gravity of the situation, they all burst out laughing at her untimely use of the phrase made famous by John McEnroe. Mouse calmed first. 'Oh shit, Elaine. Shit, shit, shit.' She knew Elaine wouldn't lie about something like this, so despite her love for Guy, Mouse didn't ask the question. 'I need a drink. Let's go out.'

'Are you sure?' Grace looked at them both. Mouse's emotions were all over the place and Elaine's accent was becoming broader with every sentence. A sure sign she was upset.

'I need to talk to Guy about this but he's thousands of miles away, so I can't. I'm not sure whether I can write to him about it either,' she thought for a moment. 'It's not something the Guy I love would do.'

'I'm sorry.'

'Don't be, Elaine. You were in a lose, lose situation. So thanks for telling me,' her voice was flat. 'When you told me that you didn't go ahead with your application because there weren't enough females in your Corps, that was a lie?'

'Yes it was. In fact Gaynor, one of ours, is already doing the job, though I'm not supposed to know that. …' Her voice trailed off as she saw her friend's reaction.

'Gaynor?' It wasn't a popular name so Mouse voiced her concerns. 'Would that happen to be the same Gaynor that Guy was seeing before we got together?'

'Yup. But obviously they're history.'

The mention of Gaynor's name had distracted Mouse from the fact that Elaine had lied again. 'Of course they are. Are we going for that drink now, or what?'

They carried on the conversation in the bar. The night wasn't going as Mouse had expected. The shine had been taken off their reunion and she needed time to think things through. She was concerned about the way Guy had treated Elaine and also troubled to discover that he could eventually be working in highly stressful situations with an ex girlfriend. The others had hardly touched their lagers and her vodka and tonic had gone flat. Mouse gave it a shuggle, to no avail. 'Do you mind if we call it a night. I need to think…'

'What do you think…?'

'This changes things, Elaine. But I love Guy and I'm sure he had his reasons.'

'But…' she stopped, knowing she'd said enough for one night. 'See you in the morning?'

'Of course. Shall we go out for breakfast?'

Happy that she was at least trying to lighten the mood, they agreed to meet outside the accommodation at nine o'clock. They hugged as if it was the end, not the beginning of the weekend, and said their goodnights.

On the walk back to their accommodation, Grace wanted to know what to expect the following day. 'Are you going to share your suspicions about Fay Anderson and the Hoskings fella?'

'It's not *my suspicions*, Grace.'

'OK, I…'

'I know for a fact that Guy set Hoskings up. Woody told me. I've worked with him for ages. He overhead Guy arranging it, and there's no way Woody would lie to me. I'm making the assumption that Guy wanted Fay Anderson to pay for her part in Mouse being bust, but can't prove that.'

'Why didn't Woody report Guy?'

'Two reasons. Firstly, Hoskings is a mean bastard and isn't popular and secondly, Guy would have covered his tracks and I take it nobody would admit their part in the events, even if Woody knew who had helped him.'

That didn't make it right, but Grace let it go. 'OK, but you can't seriously think that Guy was able to make a classified document disappear from a four star headquarters, and then magic it back again? Come on?'

'That is a stretch I know but...'

Grace interrupted. 'And If Guy actually set them both up, why hasn't he done anything about Sergeant Jones?'

'OK, let's take Fay Anderson out of the picture, maybe I'm getting a bit carried away here. As far as Sergeant Jones is concerned, she's as thick as mince. She's failed her education three times already and is still an acting sergeant. There's no way she's going any further so he doesn't need to do anything.'

'How do you know all this?'

'Because I'm a bloody copper and if I want to know something, there are ways and means.'

'Ooooh, check you out,' Grace laughed. 'Are you going to share any of this with Mouse?'

'I am and not only because of the promise I made to her.'

'Go on.' Grace frowned.

'I'm going to use the Hoskings business as leverage for Guy to give me back the note I wrote and to stop him from scuppering my chances at special duties.'

'Oh Christ,' Grace stopped walking and put an arm on Elaine so she stopped too. She could understand Elaine's reasons but wasn't entirely comfortable with her actions.

'So he's blackmailing you and you are going to do the same to him?'

Elaine nodded gravely.

'And are you going to explain that to Mouse too?'

'I'm not sure. Look, from her point of view the fella she loves is thousands of miles away and one of her bessies is going to blackmail him. How do you think that's going to go?'

Grace ignored the question. 'This is turning into some weekend eh?'

They entered their accommodation and said goodnight. Elaine hoped she'd be able to get some sleep, but very much doubted it.

As much as they tried to put the previous night's conversation behind them, it was the elephant in the room as they made their way to Monchengladbach in Grace's car. They sat outside one of the cafés in the Alte Markt, and ordered hot drinks and a continental breakfast. It wasn't yet ten o'clock but the place was bustling. The girls relaxed as they people watched. Some people sported fashion perms and were stylishly dressed in designer t-shirts, leather jackets and skinny jeans. The girls discreetly took the mickey out of those who dressed in outfits that apparently passed for local fashion.

'I get that older blokes dress like that, but girls in their twenties?!' Grace nodded towards a good-looking woman who was wearing a short denim skirt and t-shirt, with ankle socks and sandals. 'Doesn't she have a mirror at home?' They laughed and relaxed into the easy banter that defined their friendship. They kept the conversation light during the delicious breakfast. Having had all night to think it over, Mouse wanted to finish the previous day's discussion and suggested they go to the Schloss in Rheydt. It wasn't as nice as the one in Wickrath and she would have loved to take her friends there, but wasn't sure whether KC had returned from exercise. Even though Gloria said he had never been there, and he had probably moved back into single accommodation by now, Mouse didn't want to risk it. She was still terrified of seeing him and planned to tell Elaine and Grace the whole story when the time felt right.

They found a bench next to the large pond. Mouse had brought a few of their breakfast rolls with her and threw some of the bread to a family of ducks.

They all stood up at the same time, without saying a word. None thought it strange; they were pretty much tuned into each other. The sun disappeared behind a cloud and the bright day turned dull. *Just like my mood* thought Mouse as they went to walk along the path. A good walk and nature could usually lift her spirits, but not today. Mouse knew her friend's mannerisms well enough to know she was nervous, so knew there was more to come.

'Shall we get this over and done with, Elaine? What else is there?'

'I'm going to stay and feed the ducks for a while,' said Grace. 'I'll catch up with you in a bit.'

Elaine gave her a grateful look and walked away with Mouse.

'Do you really want to do special duties?'

'Yup.'

'I've thought about what you said last night and I can't get my head around it. For Guy to do something like that, he must really think you're a danger to others.'

Elaine tried to see it from her friend's point of view, but it was a challenge. 'Really, Mouse? Is that what you think? Seriously?'

'To be honest I don't know what to think. I'm having trouble getting my head around the situation and it seems to me that I have to side with one of you. You can't both be right.'

'I know it's hard for you to take in, but I really want a shot at special duties. You know it's something I've wanted to do for a while.'

'Are you going to call Guy's bluff?'

Elaine didn't reply straight away.

'What aren't you telling me, Elaine?'

'At times I think you should be a copper. I work with a bloke called Woody. He's straight as a dye and I'd trust him with my life if it came to it.' She could see that Mouse was about to interrupt. 'Let me explain. Woody overheard Guy arranging to set up a bloke called Corporal Hoskings. Name ring a bell with you?'

Mouse grimaced. 'He's the bastard who said he saw me hitting Jonesy.'

'The one and same. So Hoskings is found with some dodgy stuff and is done for thieving. He denied it. He's not a good bloke, but he's not a thief either. Well not in this case anyway. Guy set him up.'

She waited for Mouse to deny it but was surprised when her comments met with silence. 'Well?' Elaine broke the silence.

'When Guy came here to see me, I told him what I'd heard. He looked pretty smug when he said *two down, one to go.* I asked him if he'd had anything to do with it and he told me that he hadn't, it was karma. He could see I would have been pissed off if he'd admitted it.'

'Oh shit!'

'Oh shit indeed.'

'What are...'

'What I'm going to do, Elaine, is enjoy the rest of the weekend with you both. I don't want anything else to spoil it.

Grace watched as her two best friends walked ahead. She hoped they could sort out their differences, but very much doubted it. She wondered for a moment why they hadn't noticed anything different about her. Especially Mouse who was usually very perceptive. Her news was just going to have to wait but Grace didn't know how much longer she could keep it bottled up. She hadn't yet decided what to do about it either. She sighed and a passing couple gave her a sympathetic look. This was enough to make her get a grip. The weekend wasn't about her, it was about Mouse and Elaine trying to reach an understanding and for them all to have a good time. Grace was probably being overly optimistic with the latter. More heavy clouds had gathered and there was no chance of the sun putting in another appearance. She hurried to catch up with her friends.

*****

All the secrets were now out in the open. Elaine had confirmed her course of action but Mouse was still undecided about what she should do. She loved Guy with all her heart, but there was a line between having a lover who protected and supported her, and one who controlled her. Memories of her time with KC came flooding back. She knew Guy was a much better man than KC would ever be, but he'd just assumed that he could control her life and the people around her. Not only that, he seemed to think he could make decisions about other people's futures as well. She had a lot to think about.

Despite their pessimism during the revelations that Friday, Mouse was certain that if they could get through this, they would be able to overcome anything. Grace was in her normal role of pacifier and peacekeeper and had been the voice of reason. When the conversation between Elaine and Mouse had been heated Grace had skilfully calmed the situation and put them back on track.

Friday afternoon passed pleasantly and the girls were in the Marley, to see the act and have fun at the disco. The Combined Services Entertainment organisation had booked Stan Boardman to do a stint. Spike was with them, which meant that talk of any touchy subjects or their secrets was taboo. Grace wasn't sure if they'd really enjoyed the comedy or whether they'd needed some lighthearted entertainment to take their minds off the serious issues they'd had to deal with. Whatever it was, they all let their hair down. The disco started and as soon as Mouse heard *Get Down on It,* she couldn't help herself.

'Come on you lot,' she stood up and writhed around her chair. 'Let's dance.'

Elaine and Spike declined. Just like a lot of blokes, alcohol gave them the confidence they needed to dance, and they hadn't yet had enough. Grace was up for it so joined her friend under the shiny silver ball. Mouse closed her eyes for a second and let the rhythm take her. Grace was a little more self-conscious. She watched her friend and wished she could lose herself in the music along with her.

The rest of the night was spent drinking, dancing, drinking. It was exactly like the old days when they could have innocent fun together, before life took over and complicated matters.

The Friday night set the pattern for the rest of the weekend. Spike had been a bit grumpy because she was on duty and couldn't join them every day, but Mouse was glad to spend time alone with Elaine and Grace. Monday came around far too quickly. By the time they said goodbye, Mouse hadn't confided her fears about KC, Grace hadn't told them her news and Elaine's emotions were all over the place. Spike came to say goodbye but sensed the atmosphere and didn't have a clue what was going on. She took Elaine's contact details and hoped to hear from her again.

*****

Mouse went into work early on the Tuesday as was her wont after being away. She hated having a backlog of work so being in before everyone else gave her a chance to catch up and to check her in-tray. She looked at her desk and wondered if a paper monster had thrown up over it. Tackling the mess, she was glad to be busy so she wouldn't have to think about her personal problems. It was still quiet and Major Best arrived earlier than she expected. He called her into his office before anyone else arrived.

'This is Staff Sergeant Wilson's last day with us, Corporal Warbutton, though he doesn't know it yet.' He explained that enough evidence had been gathered to charge him. 'He's been filming his wife in, err, compromising situations with other men and selling the videos.' He was embarrassed about discussing such matters with his female clerk and coughed to hide his discomfort.

'As it turns out, we don't need any help from you on this. Ten minutes after he comes into the office I want you to make yourself scarce, Corporal Warbutton. It's not going to be pleasant.'

Mouse considered whether she should now tell her boss about the incident in Aldershot.

'Everything OK?'

'Yes, sir,' she answered, deciding not to spill the beans about trouser-gate as they had enough to charge Staff Wilson and she didn't need the hassle. 'Coffee?'

As she waited for the kettle to boil, she thought it might be good to hang around, but out of sight of the main event. She smiled to herself in the knowledge that for the first time in ages, there was going to be a major drama that had absolutely nothing to do with her.

Chapter 12

Graham had been warned for a tour of duty in the Falklands. Now that the war was over a permanent garrison was to be established on the islands so more troops were to be deployed. He was told that he would be away for six months and didn't yet know whether he would be entitled to R&R, midway through the tour. The news had made Grace's problem more urgent and they were about to spend a week on leave together, before Graham was kitted out and flown to the other side of the world. Grace was terrified and still undecided what to do, so wanted to see Graham's reaction before she made up her mind. She didn't want a long journey to cut into their time together so opted to fly. As she came through customs, he was at the gate. He picked her up and swung her around.

'I'm…' she started but he silenced her with a lingering kiss that held promise of what was to come later when they were alone. Others waiting for their loved ones smiled, feeling the joy of the young couple. He held her away when they came up for air, wanting to take in every inch of her. She'd put on a little weight but he didn't mention it; he wasn't stupid. Grace smiled and wiped away the tears that wouldn't stop. She laughed, embarrassed.

'Oh, Gracie, don't cry. We've got a whole week together before I go.'

'It's not that, it's…' she shook her head, not sure if this was the right place to give him the news.

'Come on,' Graham threw her bag over his shoulder and took her hand. 'Let's get a drink before we go to the car. Then you can tell me all about it.' They were spending their week at Butlins. The chalet would be private enough for them to enjoy each other's company and within the limited budgets of junior NCOs. Graham didn't want any distractions when Grace told him her news, especially if it was what he suspected.

They found a quiet booth in a local pub. 'Lager, Gracie?' She declined and asked for orange juice, making him think he was right. He took a sip from his pint then put both drinks on the table. Sitting down, Graham put one arm around Grace and pulled her into him. He took her hand in his and smiled his encouragement. 'Tell me, Gracie.'

Feeling a little calmer, she knew she'd been wrong to doubt him, even though she hadn't said it out loud. 'I'm pregnant.' She closed her eyes, and then risked opening one.

'Yes!' he freed an arm and punched his fist in the air.

Some of the other customers looked in the direction of the shout, but Graham didn't care. He gently pulled her to him and held her as if she were made of porcelain, then moved a strand of hair and put his lips to her ear. 'Will you marry me, Gracie?' They broke apart and looked at each other. More tears came and she wiped them away roughly. 'Yes. Oh yes, Graham. I'll have to leave the Army and we'll be totally skint. And what if we fall out or you don't love me when I get fat…'

He put a finger to her lips. 'I'll always love you. You've made me the happiest man alive.'

'Will you still have to go to the Falklands?'

He laughed. 'You know what the Army's like. What do you think?'

She didn't answer. They finished their drinks and made their way to the car, planning their future as they did so. 'I'll have to write to my OC for permission to marry, and you'll have to tell your unit and arrange your discharge. I don't think we'll be able to do it before I go. Is that OK?'

'I'm not telling them until after the three month point. Apparently, anything could happen before then.'

He remembered his mother's miscarriage, but Grace was young and fit and he told her so, adding. 'But whatever you want to do is fine by me.' Another squeeze and kiss proved to Grace exactly how happy Graham was. People would gossip about her bump and the fact that she was single but she didn't care. Graham would be gone within two weeks and there wasn't enough time to sort anything before he left. She was just glad that her mind was made up. She was keeping the baby, getting married and leaving the Army. By keeping the baby she would have to leave the Army anyway, rules was rules. It was all pretty scary but she didn't have to do it on her own. 'We'll have to phone our families this week. And I want to tell Mouse and Elaine.'

'So I'm really the first to know? I thought you might have told the girls.'

She explained what had happened during the long weekend with her friends.

'But Guy's a good bloke.'

'I know. He's got your sister's best interests at heart but he's gone totally over the top.'

'What's Mouse going to do?'

'You know she's still mad about him, Gray, but she's also mad at him. She's not going to mention it in her letters, he's out there amongst God only knows what and has enough to worry about. Their reunion will be interesting, to say the least.'

'Hmm.' Graham was worried about his sister but wouldn't let it take the shine off his time with Grace.

'Please don't mention it to Guy if you see him in the Falklands.'

'Of course not. I'll have a chat with Mouse after we've given her our news. Is she OK?'

'Yeah, sort of, besides for all this stuff with Guy.'

'Did she tell you about KC and that lass you all know from training?'

They talked about KC and Gloria and agreed that KC was the type to want revenge. The fact that Mouse hadn't discussed it with Elaine and Grace was measure of how much she was occupied with thoughts of Guy. They were both worried about her.

'Surely KC wouldn't be stupid enough to have another go at her?' said Grace.

They both hoped so but neither really believed it.

*****

KC was sick and tired of staring at the walls in his bunk. He felt the anger bubbling away but knew he couldn't afford to get into any more trouble. His sergeant major had told him he was lucky to still be wearing a stripe. He also told him that their OC had recently had woman trouble - his wife had left him for another man – so he had sympathised with KC and been lenient. Consequently, KC had taken the extra duties and other punishment, and arranged for the repairs of his married quarter, before handing it back to the Army. He was totally skint. The other lads in the squadron loved him because if there was a shitty task to be carried out, he was the man to do it. He'd had to agree not to pursue Gloria, except through the letters sent by his or her legal representative. KC didn't contest the divorce so it would be relatively straightforward. He had to let it go for now and it was this injustice, coupled with the knowledge that Mouse must have been involved, that fuelled his fury. He put on his sports kit and decided to take it out on the punch bag in the gym. The chief muscle buster told him he had potential as a boxer and KC enjoyed working the punch bag, imagining whose face it could be. When not doing that he allowed himself a few pints in the top bar. He'd made a couple of new mates there while playing table tennis and pool. When he felt really down he went to the coffee bar where the WRVS woman, Daisy was based. She was a good laugh and she'd somehow managed to get him to talk about his problems. He didn't know how she'd done it but he'd actually felt better for talking to her. It didn't alter the fact that he would get his own back on Gloria and Mouse, no matter how long it took.

*****

The days were getting shorter and autumn was just around the corner. Mouse started to relax. Staff Wilson had been removed from post and was being court martialled along with his wife. Details were in *The Sixth Sense*. Rumour had it that the chain of command had intervened so that the newspaper didn't show overly graphic photographs of Staff's wife, who was a WRAC sergeant, in certain outfits and positions with other soldiers. Notwithstanding the nature of their work, the office was a lot happier without Staff Sergeant Wilson. Mouse hadn't been bothered by KC, but had heard from Gloria who now had a job at the Marine Training Centre in Torpoint. She wondered if it were possible that KC had let it go and had moved on? She very much doubted it but lived in hope. Graham had settled into his job in the Falklands and she was going to be an auntie in six months or so. The letters from Guy were filled with his undying love and Mouse re-read them until they started to disintegrate. She hadn't forgotten his controlling and worrying behaviour but knew his motivation couldn't be faulted, even though his actions could. Since Staff Wilson's departure, Mouse had been given additional responsibilities in the office. She'd accidentally on purpose overheard a conversation between Major Best and his boss, Lieutenant Colonel Greaves. Major Best was pushing for her promotion and Mouse knew he was able to talk the colonel around to his own way of thinking, and that meant a cracking report in her twenty sixty six if she were lucky. She'd be so chuffed if she could give Guy news of her promotion. He'd been promoted to sergeant recently so she would only be one rank behind him. Elaine was hoping to get promoted that year too though Mouse thought she was being overly optimistic. Still, promotion would see Mouse ahead of her peer group and she didn't want to miss out.

103

Guy looked at his chuff chart on the wall. He'd started it three days after the war ended. And now, almost three months later, he was going home. The Argie POWs, paras and marines in various guises, penguins and many depictions of the local population had been sketched and then crossed off as each day ended. Home was wherever Mouse happened to be. He didn't want them to spend any time with his mother so his plan was to visit Yorkshire and stay overnight before meeting Mouse off her flight. He knew the kids loved to see him and would feel guilty if he didn't visit. He also needed to ensure that Mrs Jarvis had everything she needed – if he could do anything to make her and his siblings' lives more pleasant, he would do his best. Guy had already set up regular payments to Mrs Jarvis's bank account and knew she loved his brothers and sisters. Now that he was a senior-NCO, he could afford to send a bit more home. If - no he assured himself - when Mouse agreed they could set a date for their wedding, they could arrange to have the kids for the occasional weekend when she returned from Germany and Guy from Northern Ireland. He hadn't expected to be encouraged to carry on with his special duties application so quickly after returning from the Falklands, but it was something he really wanted to do, so couldn't complain.

The first part of the flight home was from Stanley to Ascension. While on the thirteen- hour journey in the Hercules, Guy was beginning to wonder if a boat trip would have been better. The noise was deafening and the seats uncomfortable. The word seat was a slight exaggeration thought Guy as he looked around. The metal frames against the side of the aircraft were covered in webbing and a strap, and Guy, along with eight other passengers, was strapped in. The reason there wasn't more passengers was due to two soldiers being CASEVACED, not casualties of war, but of road traffic accidents, and the stretchers they occupied were securely fastened. Medical staff checked various pieces of equipment and Guy watched the nurse who had informed them all in no uncertain terms, that she was the senior officer on the flight. The doctor was a young captain and even he seemed irritated by her. They were only four hours into the flight and she had already annoyed the majority of passengers by giving unnecessary orders and making an uncomfortable flight even worse. Guy knew something was going on by the whispering and chuckling of a few of the other soldiers. He watched as the major approached the toilet, a rudimentary facility with just a curtain pulled around for privacy. One of the soldiers nudged another then suddenly, the toilet curtain dropped to the ground and Major Pearson appeared in all her glory, with her knickers around her ankles. They all laughed as she attempted to pull up her knickers with one hand while trying to protect her modesty with the other. Guy saw a soldier attempt to conceal the string he'd pulled to bring down the curtain. After she'd finished, she stomped along the aisle looking like she were about to have a toddler tantrum.

'Sergeant Halfpenny.' She shouted above the noise of the aircraft.

'Yes, ma'am.' Guy tried to make it sound genuine but it came out all wrong.

'Don't take that attitude with me.'

'How can I help you, ma'am?' This time he managed to pull it off and she appeared to calm a little.

'You can help, Sergeant Halfpenny, by investigating this incident and identifying the culprit or culprits, so they can receive their just deserts.'

He was about to respond disrespectfully but saw the look on her face. The bloody woman was bonkers so he'd have to box clever.

'Of course.' Guy unstrapped himself and made his way to the toilet. As he passed the soldier who'd hidden the string, he winked conspiratorially. The man looked down, not giving the game away. A few minutes later Guy approached Major Pearson. 'It appears that the curtain fell, ma'am. I guess you were just unlucky.'

She blustered and shook her head. 'You haven't heard the last of this, Sergeant Halfpenny, nor the rest of you.' She stormed off to check on one of her patients. Poor sod, thought Guy. The rest of the flight passed uneventfully. Guy disembarked the Hercules and was relieved to be getting on the VC 10. The seats faced the rear of the aircraft but it still felt like luxury compared to the last flight and the engine noise was quiet enough for a comfortable sleep, which is exactly what Guy did on and off during the nine hour journey.

Despite sleeping on the plane he was knackered by the time he arrived in Yorkshire. His mother had used his return as an excuse for the kids to stay off school and none of the four had argued. Guy guessed that the plumber wasn't about as soon as he entered the house. The happy atmosphere of kids doing what they wanted while his useless mother lazed about was preferable to the discipline instilled by the plumber. They were all in their pajamas and dressing gowns and the house was in chaos. Guy attacked the mess in the kitchen but stopped when the doorbell rang. Mrs Jarvis looked sprightlier than he remembered. She had a twinkle in her eye and he wasn't convinced that it came from looking after his brothers and sisters. Guy made his mother a coffee and offered to take them all out, along with Mrs Jarvis. His mother declined, telling him she needed a break and some time on her own.

'Take the kids out, son.' He made her a chicken curry flavour pot noodle at her request. His mother carried on flicking through the pages of her magazine so Guy stood in front of her, until she at least acknowledged his presence. 'Thanks, son,' she didn't even look up. I'll see you in a bit.' He was lucky, she hadn't said a word to Mrs Jarvis.

Guy wondered why he was disappointed. He should have known better by now but there was always that shred of hope that absence might make the heart grown fonder. It made the hair grow longer in her case, but that was about it.

They went to the park and each of his siblings was vying for his attention. When Mr Barston arrived, the kids welcomed him like an old friend and Guy raised an eyebrow to Mrs Jarvis. She declined to comment but they flirted like smitten teenagers and Guy loved the fact that she had found companionship, and maybe something else, in her later years. The main thing was that, the day he was home the kids seemed happy and Guy was giving them everything he could, except his time. He was starting to become fidgety and Mrs Jarvis let him off the hook.

'Your brother has to go back to his Army duties now, say goodbye everyone.'

'Did you kill any Argies?' asked Michael.

Guy rubbed his brother's head, and then pulled the hood of his jacket down over his face to wind him up. They play fought for a minute or so.

'So did you?'

'No I didn't. I took lots of guns and other weapons off the Argies, but they'd stopped fighting by then.'

'What did you do to them?'

'We locked them up so they couldn't hurt anyone, then we sent them back home.'

He nodded his head, seeming satisfied by his brother's answer.

'Can we feed the ducks?' Asked his youngest sister and a request for ice cream followed.

Guy said his goodbyes and left, feeling guilty. He always felt bad when leaving his family. Probably because he remembered what he'd had to endure. He hoped his brothers and sisters were spared the same but, by the look of Michael, he'd had to assume responsibility for the rest of them. Guy thanked Mrs Jarvis and wished her and Mr Barston well. She actually blushed. He made his way to the train station where he collected his kit from left luggage. He'd travel to the airport and meet Mouse off her flight, before they went to pick up the hire car he'd pre-ordered. The anticipation of seeing her at long last was almost too much to bear.

*****

Within an hour of the pains starting, Grace knew she'd lost the baby. She tried to tell herself that they would have others in the future, but couldn't help feeling guilty. She wondered if things might have been different had she stopped work, drank less coffee, slept more or ate more tomatoes. It was three days before Grace could bring herself to tell anyone. She reported to the medical centre. The nurse was sympathetic and said she knew what Grace was going through. Grace doubted that. How could anyone know how she felt? Graham had so been looking forward to having this baby. In a moment of doubt she wondered if he would still want to marry her. She knew she was being stupid but her emotions were all over the place. Grace had to speak to Mouse so called her after leaving the medical centre. She knew it wouldn't be an easy call.

'Hi, Grace. I'm really busy. Can I call you back?'

'Mouse, I need to speak to you.'

Mouse knew from her tone that it wasn't good news and her stomach lurched. 'What's happened?'

Before Grace had a chance to answer she heard somebody speaking to Mouse in the background.

'I'm sorry, sir, but I have to take this call. I'll be in as soon as I've finished.'

'I'm not getting you in the shit am I?' Asked Grace.

'No.' Mouse lied. 'Tell me, please.'

107

'I've lost our baby. Graham's going to be devastated. I'm...'

She sobbed into the receiver and Mouse resisted the urge to say that there'd be others. It was probably the last thing she wanted to hear.

'I'm so sorry, Grace. I know how much you were both looking forward to being parents. Can you get some time off and take a break or something?'

'That's the last thing I want to do. I so wish Graham was here.'

'Well, I can relate to that.' Mouse didn't want to remind Grace that she was flying to the UK that evening, but her friend remembered.

'I hope you have a lovely time. But why on earth are you going to the Scottish Highlands?'

They both chuckled. 'I know. It seemed like a good idea at the time. Perhaps the weather will be kind to us.'

'Yeah, and the Pope's a Protestant.'

Mouse could hear that Grace was trying her hardest to sound like her usual upbeat self. She wasn't fooled.

'Is there anything I can do to help you?'

'Nothing's going to make me feel better. I haven't even told my parents yet so there's no point talking to them about it. I'll have to write to Graham, otherwise he'll expect...' she sobbed again. 'Sorry. It'll be a shock when he sees me if I don't tell him. It seems wrong writing about it though.'

'I'm so sorry. I know you and Graham are strong enough to come through this.'

They talked for a little longer, and then hung up. Mouse was gutted for her friend and her brother and worried about Grace. She'd offered to cut short her leave with Guy to spend some time with her. Grace had declined and Mouse admitted to herself that she was relieved. It might be selfish but she wanted to spend as much time as she could with Guy, before he was off again to train for his next job. Their reunion wasn't going to be easy because she was determined to put a stop to his controlling behaviour. She would get together with Grace the weekend after returning from the UK, even if it meant travelling there and back on the same day.

Grace felt slightly better having talked to Mouse so decided to write to Graham there and then. She'd put it off for long enough and it was only fair to tell him as soon as possible. An hour later she returned from the post box, exhausted. The block was quiet and she turned everything off in her bunk, curled up onto her bed and cried herself to sleep.

*****

Boxing was a release for KC. Each time he punched the bag, he imagined he was hitting Gloria or Mouse. Each time he stepped into the ring one of their faces replaced that of his opponent. Once he started he found it difficult to stop, which was the only criticism from his trainer, Big Al Etherington. The old sergeant was an ex Army champ and was surprisingly light on his feet for such a big fella. He watched the angry lance corporal with interest, and a lot of frustration.

'Who's wound you up today, Cooke? Take a break and calm yourself down.' He swiped his protégé with an old towel.

He thought about KC's progress. From the time he'd been brought to his attention in the inter-unit championships, his progress had been rapid. He'd been a rough diamond but Al had smoothed the edges and Cooke was now a talented Middleweight boxer. What he hadn't been able to do was rid him of his anger. Al knew the man had issues and it was pretty obvious that he wanted to inflict pain on someone, so far Cooke had controlled his anger but Al had the feeling he had a loose cannon on his hands. The man in charge of the Army Boxing Team, Captain Grant, had been fighting the Argies and was still in the Falklands. It had come as a surprise to Al and the current squad that the Inter-Services Boxing Competition was still going ahead. He thought most of the Naval Boxing team, made up mainly of Royal Marines, would still be in the Falklands but was told that wasn't the case. Those way above him deemed that it would be good for morale for the boxing to take place. Unusually for Al, he was undecided about one of the potential squad members. Should he include KC or not? On a good day the man would be an asset with a strong chance of winning. He sensed that it wouldn't take much to tip him over the edge, and then Christ only knew what might happen. He wondered whether to speak to the boxing director, Lieutenant Colonel Barclay, but unlike Captain Grant, the colonel wanted the credit with none of the hassle. Al had to make the decision.

'Am I in, sarge?' Cooke's question broke his train of thought.

'Aye, you're in, son. If you let me down I'll rip your head off and shit in it. Understand?'

It seemed pretty clear to KC. 'Perfectly, sarge. I won't let you down.' He believed it too.

*****

Another airport, another reunion. Mouse dropped her bags as soon as she saw him and stood to attention.

'Congratulations, sarge.'

Guy laughed and embraced her. He couldn't believe he was holding her in his arms. This was sanity. This was real. When he touched her and breathed in the apple scent of her hair and felt her soft curves, the world seemed sane. He didn't have to worry about anyone pulling a gun or knife on him. She made him feel normal and he never wanted to let her go.

Mouse felt loved and secure. Nobody had come close to evoking the feelings she felt for this man. At times she didn't like some of the things he did, but she loved him with all her heart and couldn't imagine life without him. Besides for that, being with him brought her world alive. Colours were more vibrant and sounds more distinctive. Nature seemed nearer. It was as if everything made sense and fitted together exactly as it should. In her world life and love were never perfect, but Mouse was sure this was the closest she would ever get to perfection and she was happy. Gloriously, sing out loud happy.

'Shall we get the car?'

'Hmmm.' She could have stayed in his embrace forever, in their own bubble, while everyone around them got on with their own business.

'We'll get cramp if we stay here, or maybe die of old age.'

They still held each other and neither made an effort to move.

The last passengers from her flight had passed with their luggage and a man and woman with brushes and carts appeared, collecting all the rubbish. They moved out of their bubble and rejoined reality.

'OK,' Mouse smiled lazily. 'Let's get the car.'

She didn't travel lightly but was able to hang onto Guy while he wheeled her case and carried her rucksack, so she only had her handbag to think about.

The car was a light blue Fiat Strada. Before departing for the Falklands, Mrs Jarvis had told Guy that money was tight. He'd sold his beloved Capri and given her the money to buy some

110

clothes and treats for the kids. Mrs Jarvis knew not to mention it to his mother. Guy had loved his car but knew he wouldn't have been able to cope with the guilt of seeing his brothers and sisters in tatters. There was nothing to spend his pay on in the Falklands so he had enough to show Mouse a good time while they were on leave. Mouse had been a saver since earning her first wage and it was a source of pride to her that she didn't need to rely on her parents or anyone else if she needed anything. If she could afford something she wanted, she would buy it, if she didn't have the cash she would save until she did. It simply did not occur to her to buy something hire purchase, or on the never, never as they called it.

'Do you want to drive, or shall I?'

The rental man looked at Mouse as if she had two heads, but Guy just laughed. 'Are you trying to tell me something?'

She explained that she'd now passed her test and had a little car of her own, she'd wanted to surprise him so had left it out of her letters. He told her about the lack of the usual celebrations when he'd been promoted. They caught up on life in general before Guy asked. 'Is there anything else I need to know since I've been away?'

They were now on the road, putting some miles between them and the airport.

'What you should know, is that I'm not spending our first night together in almost six months, in a tent out in the Scottish wilds.'

'But you enjoyed camping last time we went.' Seeing the look on her face, he decided not to take the wind-up any further. He laughed. 'Only kidding, sweetheart.

'Nor in a back of a rental car either.'

'Ditto. That's why I've booked us into…'

'Where?'

'You'll find out shortly.'

She poked and prodded him as much as she could while he was driving, to no avail. 'So your training means you won't talk.' Mouse tickled him but he swerved dangerously which freaked them both.

'Sorry. I'll wait and see.' She was happy just to be in his company and laid her head on his arm. Guy drove the twenty or so miles to their hotel.

Far enough off the main road to give the impression it was deep in the countryside, the imposing eighteenth century building had been recently refurbished. The rooms were a fair size with large beds and were warm – he knew that was a must for Mouse. The weather in September could be unpredictable so he'd had to cover all bases. Guy had heard about the hotel from an officer's conversation in the cookhouse. If it was good enough for Major Watts and his wife, he hoped it would be good enough for Mouse. He wanted this night to be perfect so had phoned and told them his requirements. The receptionist had expected Mr and Mrs Halfpenny to be older but hid her surprise. They had all sorts of people staying at their hotel and were required to accept the money and not to judge. It wasn't always easy to do. The giggling from Mrs Halfpenny made it even more difficult.

Their bodies did most of the talking that night. Guy's nightmare woke Mouse when it was still dark. She had no idea of the time, only knowing it was stupid o'clock and neither of them had had enough sleep. As his body shook and he called out, Mouse held him tightly and murmured reassurances, even though he probably wouldn't hear her. Eventually he calmed down and she went back to a disturbed sleep, dreaming of being attacked by KC.

Mouse awoke suddenly and tried to shake the dream from her head. She was with the man she loved and didn't want to spend any time thinking about the fuckwit that she might have married, and who was still the bane of her life.

After a delicious and what she considered posh breakfast, they left the hotel and carried on the road north. The roads weren't too congested and it was a good time to talk. As much as she loved him, Mouse needed to outline the boundaries. There was only one way she knew how to broach the subject.

'You know I love you, Guy.'

'Yes?' He'd heard the *but* in her statement. Guy didn't see the need to discuss everything. They loved each other and everything else would fall into place as far as he was concerned.

'I can't cope with you keeping things from me.' She was twiddling her hands and looking at them.

'Like what?'

So he wanted her to say it out loud. 'Like punishing that Hoskings fella for what he did. I know you want to protect me but you should have spoken to me about it first.'

'And you would have agreed to what I did?'

'No, of course not.'

'So?'

'So I would have talked you out of it and karma would have sorted him out, like it did for Fay Anderson.'

'Karma.' Guy shook his head. This was exactly the reason that she needed to be looked after.

'Yes, Guy, karma. What goes around comes around and all that.'

'Mouse,' he indicated and pulled into the slow lane away from any other traffic. 'Just think of it as karma, but it's come early.' He slapped her thigh. 'They both only got what they deserved, sweetheart, but by different means.'

'I know that. I appreciate you fighting my battles but you were totally out of order and I want you to promise you'll never do anything like that again. Do you promise?'

'Sweetheart, it's my job to look after you and I'll do that any way I can.'

'That's not looking after me, Guy. That's taking the law into your own hands like you're some sort of vigilante.' She was struggling to make him understand and shouted her frustration. 'It's not normal behaviour.'

'And it's normal behaviour to help your mate escape from your ex-fiancé?'

Her head jerked back in surprise. *How the hell did he know about that?*

'That's got nothing to do with what we're discussing, but actually, I was helping a mate to escape from domestic violence. It just happened to be from my ex.'

'Your ex who attacked you and you weren't going to tell me about it?'

Shit.

He'd deflected her concerns and the discussion carried on in a different vein, Mouse explaining that she hadn't wanted to worry him when he was going off to war. A ceasefire ensued, neither comfortable with the outcome.

After spending a memorable night in a luxuriously comfortable hotel room, Guy reluctantly admitted that perhaps camping in the middle of the countryside hadn't been one of his better ideas. Mouse had told him more than once that she would love to see the Scottish Highlands. She had some sort of romantic notion of them walking hand in hand through the heather, finding a quiet glen and making love under the starlit sky. Guy was well up for that but knew she didn't like the cold and loved her home comforts; as far as the Army provided home comforts. He also knew she was adventurous and thought she'd love the idea of this type of camping. They'd been before but at a site that had all mod cons and plenty of facilities. Now he realised he'd been way off base. Still, the decision had been made and he decided to pitch in a desolate spot in the base of a wooded valley surrounded by hills. They'd been travelling since breakfast, stopping only once for a quick bite to eat and to purchase some provisions. He knew that Mouse meant well when she decided to help him pitch the tent. Her efforts were hindering his so he decided to send her on an errand.

'I'll sort this. Can you sort the latrine please.'

'What?' she looked at him as if he was speaking Klingon.

'We need to dig a latrine. There's a spade in the boot of the car.'

She looked at their surroundings. 'You're not kidding are you?' His look answered her question. 'I'll have you know that I'm not the sort of girl who err, shits in the woods. Where's the nearest toilets?'

Guy eventually got it through to her that nature provided the toilets but they should be responsible and bury their waste. Mouse walked off in a strop with the spade.

By the time she returned, the tent was up and the double sleeping bag ready. Guy had set up the gas stove outside. A small kettle was on one ring and a pan containing food of unknown origin on the other. Filling was the best that Mouse could say about the tinned food. Curled up in the sleeping bag later, the meal had an adverse effect.

'Where'd you put the comfy bum? I need it pretty quickly.' She jumped up and ran out to the car.

Guy couldn't believe he'd forgotten something so basic. It had been on their list too. 'Sorry, sweetheart, you're going to have to find some leaves to use.'

'You have got to be kidding.' She was desperate by this stage and waddled to the poo pit as quickly as she could.

As they cuddled up in their sleeping bag later, Guy tried to get her to see the funny side. Mouse had only been able to find pine leaves and her backside was still smarting. Thinking she'd give anything for a shower, she drifted off to sleep still in her lover's arms, despite their differences.

Dreaming she was back in Germany and had been caught in the rain, Mouse opened her eyes and realised it wasn't a dream. Looking at her luminous watch told her it was just after three o'clock. The noise was coming from the tent next door. Mouse couldn't believe that in all the miles of the Scottish Highlands, German tourists had decided to pitch a tent next to theirs, and then have a party at three o'clock in the morning. The tent was waterproof until it started to rain. All their belongings were wet and so were Mouse and Guy. Before she had a chance to prod him, he opened his eyes. Without a word Guy got up and ran to the car. He brought them both dry clothes, which he'd bundled into their jackets so they didn't get wet. They emptied the tent, packing the car as quickly as they could, and then dismantled it. Guy didn't even bother having a word with the Germans – they were far too out of it by this stage. It was nearing four o'clock as they left the valley to look for somewhere else to stay. Mouse didn't know where, but knew for certain it wouldn't be bloody camping.

*****

The Army boxing team were well prepared for their first Inter-Services match. They were up against the Royal Navy and the contests were to take place at HMS Raleigh Training Centre in Torpoint, Cornwall. KC was keyed up. Fighting at middleweight, the opposition had heard of the newcomer and wanted to prove a point after their loss the previous year. The newbie was the man they all wanted to beat. They'd all warmed up and the Welterweight contest had just taken place. The Navy were winning by three bouts to nil and the crowd sounded as if they were baying for blood. KC pulled the curtain back before venturing outside. The military audience were seated in chairs around the ring. It always amazed him that the dress for these functions was mess kit for the officers and senior NCOs, long dresses for the ladies and Number Two dress for the junior ranks. They all made an effort to look their best so that they could watch blokes battering the shit out of each other.

He made his way to the ring with his seconds each side of him. One lifted the ropes making a wider gap for him to step into. KC was keyed up and confident of his own abilities. He was good and he knew it. He did a bit of fancy footwork while jabbing at an invisible opponent. Then he battered his chest like a gorilla. Some of the Navy supporters started chanting that he was going down, until their superiors told them to behave. The Army supporters were also calmed, but KC loved the attention and wound them up as much as he knew he could get away with. A look from Big Al told him to quit and he faced at his opponent. Standing a few inches taller than him with a nose that had plainly seen many boxing matches and eyes hungry for action, KC knew he'd have his work cut out. Neither man would look away first so KC was pulled to his red corner and Big Al turned him to face the crowd.

Gloria had settled into life with her brother David and sister-in-law Ellie. David had put in a good word and she was working at the Torpoint training base, administering new recruits. She wasn't a fan of boxing but they'd coerced her into watching the Navy versus Army match. They were trying to set her up with one of David's mates but Gloria told them a relationship was the last thing she was looking for at the moment. They thought they knew better so Gloria played along, up to a point. Ellie was a lot taller and a completely different shape so she'd taken Gloria to the dress hire shop in town where she'd hired a royal blue, bodice hugging dress. Ellie had lent her a crystal necklace and earrings and they'd had their hair put into French plaits that afternoon. For the first time in ages Gloria felt good about herself. They met a few of David's mates outside the gymnasium, which had been transformed into the boxing venue. David and his friends were corporals so were dressed in their smart uniforms and they escorted the ladies to their seats. Gloria had sat politely through the first three bouts, smiling and clapping in the right places. Still an Army wife in name only, she was supporting the Navy boxers along with the company she was in.

As KC looked around he did a double take. A woman in the crowd was the image of his bitch of a wife, only this one was glamorous and fit looking. As his stare lingered, he realised it was Gloria. HE felt his heart pump faster and the blood rushed to his head. He gripped the rope and had he not been wearing gloves, would have damaged the skin on his hands. Big Al noticed the change in him and followed the direction of his stare. Gloria recognised her husband at the same time and Big Al noticed her expression change from a smile to one of fear. The object of his protégé's anger became clear to him.

'Fuck,' he muttered to himself.

The bell rang. KC's world went into slow motion and the blood pounded in his ears. As he walked toward his opponent his mentor grabbed him and whispered in his ear.

'You fuck this up and you'll wish you were never born.'

KC nodded his acknowledgement but said nothing. He punched his hands together a few times and bent his head from side to side, trying to loosen the tension and refocus on his opponent. The man stared at him.

'You're going down,' he mouthed out of sight of the referee. The referee told them to shake gloves and the bell went for the bout to start.

Gloria watched in horror. Sensing her tension, Ellie looked at her sister-in-law and knew something was wrong.

'Gloria?'

'It's him.'

'David.'

'I heard.'

'No. Please don't,' said Ellie as David stood up. She put out a hand to restrain him. His two friends had heard her plea. They had no idea what was going on but knew it was trouble by the look on his face.

'Whatever it is, mate, now's not the time.'

Ellie agreed with him and David looked at all of them. Gloria was looking at the floor and refused to meet his eyes. David would sort her husband, but knew she wouldn't want to see it. He sat back down and watched.

Fuelled by his rage, KC fought like a man possessed. Each punch he took appeared to have no effect and his opponent took a battering. Even the Naval supporters called for the referee to stop the bout, which he did halfway through the second round. The brave seaman staggered about like a drunk, telling anyone who would listen that he was fine; he clearly wasn't. The referee lifted KC's arm into the air and the Army supporters went mental. He'd saved the day and it wasn't going to be a complete whitewash. KC's unsmiling eyes scanned the crowd. He saw Gloria and her companions walking up the aisle he had walked down. Any attempt at restraint had left him and the red mist came down. He badly wanted to hurt Gloria. He jumped over the ropes and was chasing the small party up the aisle before Big Al realised his intention. The crowd watched as the Army lad ran. The party were near the exit but turned as one, the rumbling of the audience alerting them to something wrong.

KC's gloved fist was in the air, ready to connect with the back of Gloria's head. Her brother pushed her out of the way but couldn't avoid the punch. Stunned, he shook his head, thankful that the man hadn't thought to remove his boxing gloves. KC tried to get to Gloria but the other marines and Ellie had whisked her through the door. David knew there wasn't much time before more of his mates came to assist and before the boxer's team would get a grip of him. He could see the boxer was still out to get his sister, so grabbed him by the back of his head. Taken off balance, KC swung round. As he did so, his face connected with David's punch.

'I'm Gloria's brother. The one who's letters you returned.' He punched him again then smashed the back of his head on the door. KC could feel the dizziness taking him and slid slowly down to the floor. A crowd had gathered and Big Al worked his way through them.

'Come near Gloria again and I'll finish what I started today. Do you understand?' David wasn't one for kicking a man when he was down, and was trying his best to stay in control.

The red mist left as quickly as it arrived and KC looked into the angry face of the big marine, and the others that had formed a semi-circle around him. He wasn't sure he'd get out in one piece and his legs turned to jelly as he tried to stand.

'Out of the way.'

Everyone looked to the direction of the commanding voice.

'That's enough, son. You've made your point.' Big Al addressed David as he dragged KC to his feet. 'Come on, fuckwit. Let's get you out of here.'

The crowd laughed at the insult and the tense situation was instantly defused, as was Big Al's plan.

KC was unceremoniously forced onto the bus by his trainer and mentor. The driver was the only one on there, reading his newspaper while waiting for the boxing squad to return. With a look from Big Al he knew his presence wasn't required so folded the paper.

'I'll be having a fag outside the gym.'

'I'll give you a shout,' said Big Al as he closed the door behind the driver.

'Sit there,' He pointed to a seat towards the front of the bus. KC did as told. 'What the fuck was all that about?' He'd heard the rumours and knew the answer but wanted it from the horse's mouth.

'My wife did a runner when I was on exercise and left me to pay the debts and hand over the quarter. Then I got a letter from Army Legal telling me she wanted a divorce.'

'I feel for you, son,' said Al, drawing him in to a false sense of security. 'I take it you did absolutely nothing wrong and your wife was a complete bitch?'

'Exactly, sarge.'

'Pull the other one, Cooke, it's got bells on?' He'd met men like this before. Brought up in homes where they saw their fathers or other men beating their mothers some turned against the men. But for the most part in Big Al's experience, the majority copied the behaviour and became abusers.

'I don't understand. What do you mean, sarge?' KC looked hurt and bewildered.

'What's that funny smell? Oh I know, it's bullshit!' He forced KC into the window, his breath in his face. The younger man couldn't move.

'Remember what I said would happen if you let me down?'

KC tried to nod.

'Well you let me down tonight.'

He really looked as if he were going to rip his head off. KC swallowed and his eyes bulged. He'd heard some of the stories about their trainer and manager but had assumed they were all exaggerated. Now he wasn't sure. Terrified, he knew he'd say anything rather than face the wrath of this man. He hoped he wasn't too late.

He loosened his grip and KC had a bout of verbal diarrhoea, promising whatever he thought Big Al wanted to hear. Fed up of listening to his crap, he cuffed him, banging his head against the window. He despised cowardly men who could only feel good about themselves by beating women. If he had his way Cooke would be out of the team and he'd never have to see the pathetic creature again. He was a pragmatist and knew that Cooke could give the Army Boxing Team a great chance of glory. If he told his bosses that they should get rid of him, he was absolutely certain that they'd decline his request. He'd tried this before with a boxer who was an even sorrier excuse for a human being. So Al had to put up with having a weasel in his team. Cooke's weaknesses would eventually come to the surface. All Al could hope for was that nothing else would happen while he was in the boxing team.

*****

They'd had to wake the people who managed the caravan site in the bay near Oban. There were a number of static caravans in place and another area set aside for tourers. There was also an area for tents but Guy knew not to suggest that again. After some friendly negotiations they were given a four-berth caravan on the shingle and sand beach. It was a large park and their caravan was far enough away from the neighbours to give them plenty of privacy. It was basic but comfortable and after the rain of the night, the heavy clouds scudded away to be replaced by bright blue skies and unseasonable sunshine. They'd struck lucky, Scotland was actually set to have a late summer that year, and it coincided with their holiday.

When they weren't making love, Mouse and Guy spent their time exploring their scenic surroundings. Neither were naturephiles but both enjoyed watching the wading birds and seeing the rare glimpse of an otter. In a moment of madness, Mouse agreed to have a shot at water skiing; Guy laughed when she told him later it was the first and last time she'd do that.

The end of the holiday came all too soon and they headed south during the night, for Mouse to catch her early morning flight to Germany. She couldn't stop the tears as they hugged goodbye. Normally one to plan ahead, Guy decided to act on impulse for once.

'Marry me, Mouse.'

'What.' She laughed and cried at the same time, knowing exactly what he had said.

'I said will you marry me?'

They had issues to sort out but both knew they were made for each other.

'Of course I'll marry you, Guy.'

He squeezed her tightly. 'Right. I'll write to my CO to ask permission and you can do the same. Then you can hand in your notice...'

'Umm, no, Guy. Why would I want to hand in my notice?'

'So that we can be together when we're married, silly.' He kissed her and Mouse was considering his words as he did so.

120

'Hang on a minute. You want me to give up my career, just because we're getting married? You're kidding right?'

The look on his face told her he wasn't. Why hadn't he raised this earlier instead of now when she only had a few minutes before having to go through customs and board her flight?

'Guy, I love you and I want to spend the rest of my life with you.' Guy looked down. 'Look at me please.' He met her eyes but she didn't like what she saw in them.

'I'm not ready to give up my career. Why can't we marry and both of us have careers? It works for plenty of other women.'

'Because I want a family, Mouse, and I thought you wanted the same.'

'I do, but not just yet. We're still young, there's plenty of time.'

'You'd better go through or you'll miss your flight.'

'Don't let's leave it like this, Guy, please.'

'Just go, Mouse. We obviously need to sort our heads out and need more time to talk about this.'

Without further words they hugged and kissed one final time, each annoyed with the other. The conversation would have been different had they known what the future had in store.

Chapter 13

Graham was absolutely gutted after reading the letter from Grace. Having got used to the idea of becoming a father, it had all been taken away from him in an instant. But more importantly he was worried about the woman he adored. He was off to see his sergeant major in the hope that he could have some time off to get back to her. He was told in no uncertain terms that nobody had died and that they'd both get over it. Graham was furious and upset but could do nothing about it. He would write to her the following day when he'd calmed down.

It had been ten days since Grace had posted the letter to Graham and almost two weeks since the miscarriage. She'd expected to feel better by now but it was as if she was enveloped in an invisible cloud of fog. However much she tried, she couldn't shake off her misery and lethargy. She knew that lots of women had miscarriages. She also knew that she was perfectly fit and healthy and so was Graham, so they would be able to conceive again. The fact that she still felt depressed when she was so much luckier than others made her beat herself up and feel even worse about her situation. Mouse was just back off leave and was going to visit in two weeks but Grace didn't know how to cope with nobody to talk to in the meantime.

She still felt depressed the following day but knew she couldn't spend the whole weekend alone with her thoughts. She made her way to the stables, thinking she might feel better if she could spend some time with one of the horses. Poppy was a speckled white and grey mare. A bit nervous at times but she generally had a lovely temperament. As Grace approached her stall, Poppy scented her and whinnied in anticipation. The horse nudged her, asking for attention and looking for treats. Grace produced some apple and Poppy was in horse heaven. Just stroking and talking to her made her feel better. Gail, one of the officers' wives who volunteered in the stables most weekends, was also glad to see her.

'She could do with a bit of exercise. Fancy taking her out?'

This was an unexpected bonus. She hadn't been to the stables since discovering she was pregnant so hadn't expected to be made so welcome.

'I'd love to, Gail. And sorry I haven't been around to help just lately. It's been...'

'You don't have to explain to me. I know you Army girls have your work cut out. It's nice to see you again mind.'

They chatted amiably while getting Poppy ready. She hadn't been exercised enough and was raring to go. Grace had to rein her in until she settled.

'Give her her head, Grace when she calms down a bit. She'll love you for it.'

They waved goodbye and Grace encouraged Poppy into a gentle canter. When they'd settled into their stride, she let the horse gallop. It felt so good being out in the fresh air with the beautiful animal. She could feel the cobwebs start to lift and experienced the surge of optimism that horse riding always gave her. All would be well with the world.

Still at a gallop, they approached a gate that Poppy had jumped countless times. At the same time she was about to jump, a loud bang startled them both. Poppy stopped dead, unfortunately Grace didn't. Her world went into slow motion as she was thrown through the air. The pain as she hit the ground was the last thing Grace remembered before losing consciousness.

*****

So that Gail could close up and get ready for her dinner party that night, Grace had agreed to remove and clean Poppy's equipment on her return, to give her a good clean and check her over before putting her out in the paddock for half an hour. She would then return her to her stall and secure the stables, before leaving for the day. The married quarters were out of bounds to single personnel. Despite this Grace had agreed to call into Gail's on her way back to the block. She didn't look like a typical squaddie and had flouted the rules and had coffee with Gail before, when her husband, a major, was away. As well as fussing over her own children, Gail worried about some of the single girls she knew, even though they were in their twenties, independent and believed they were more than able to look after themselves.

Gail had expected to hear from Grace between five thirty and six o'clock. It was close to seven o'clock and she was dressed ready for the dinner party at the colonel's house. She'd never been happy in the company of sycophantic brown-nosers, but had always known it was her job to support her husband at various functions. Seeing how worried Gail was, the major knew it was no good arguing; he'd have to call Colonel Parry and give their apologies. He'd be told it was *a bad show* on Monday, but there was no way that Gail would go out until she'd heard from the lance corporal she'd befriended. Major West wondered what the world was coming to when their social life was dictated by a female junior non commissioned officer.

Alarm bells rang when Gail and her husband saw Poppy standing outside her stall, all alone. They found Grace fifteen minutes later. Major West called 112 while Gail held her hand and talked to her, even though she didn't know if she'd be heard. Grace was still unconscious when they secured her into the helicopter and flew the ninety kilometres to accident and emergency at St Cornelius Hospital. It was too early to say whether she would pull through, but she had the best team available working on her.

*****

Saturday dragged and Mouse couldn't be bothered to socialise. She wasn't in the mood for company; too busy wondering what her future had in store. Spike had asked her to go out but left her alone when she'd snapped at her, at the third time of asking. Serve her right that she was alone with the company of crappy BFBS TV, watching programmes that had shown in the UK more than two weeks ago. Mouse could only wonder why the programme schedulers thought repeats of *The Good Old Days* might appeal to a military audience, or any audience for that matter. The box was on only for the company it brought, but she couldn't even be bothered to watch rubbish television. Eventually fed up with feeling sorry for herself, she decided to plan her Sunday. She'd go to the gym where one of the wives ran an aerobics class, then pop into the office to check the contents of her in-tray. Work, better than anything else could take her mind off Guy, for a few minutes anyway.

Checking through the silent hours signals, Mouse started arranging them into piles as she read them, according to their importance. A few notified of premature births where babies were listed seriously or very seriously ill. Others where soldiers or their dependants had been granted a free passage to the UK because a parent or other close relative had been taken ill or were on the verge of dying. Then one or two signals requesting that the next of kin of soldiers who had been seriously injured in Germany, travel to see their relative as soon as possible. Such requests were only made if the injury to the individual was life threatening. In these cases the military unit would arrange accommodation, meals and transport and the Padre would provide pastoral care as required. As she was absentmindedly sorting through the signals, Mouse felt her pulse quicken as her brain recognised a regimental number. Before she had properly processed the information, she read Grace's name.

'Oh no,' she said out loud as she finished reading the signal. 'Please, no. No, no, no.' When she calmed herself down and re-read the signal, Mouse wondered whether she should contact the duty officer. She looked at the name on the list. He worked in General Staff Division 4 and would have to read the rules before doing what she asked. Hell, he might not even agree to contact her brother because Graham wasn't Grace's next of kin. There was only one thing for it. Mouse picked up the phone and dialled her boss's number. 'Sir, it's me. I need your help.'

Major Best took over on arrival at the office. He phoned the duty officer at 513 Signal Squadron, Grace's unit, to discuss the arrival of her parents. They were visiting under the DILFOR - Dangerously ill forwarding of relatives – scheme. Major Best informed him that Corporal Warbutton would arrive the following day and would accompany Grace's parents during their stay.

'Corporal Warbutton is going to be Lance Corporal Fleming's sister-in-law, so has a strong connection to the family. This is in addition to, not instead of any support your Squadron will provide,' he added to placate the duty officer. The man informed Major Best that accommodation would be organised for both Corporal Warbutton and Grace's parents and that she should report to the guardroom for further details on arrival.

When he hung up Major Best drafted a signal to the Falkland Islands, advising that compassionate leave was granted for the other Corporal Warbutton, Mouse's brother. He hoped the lad's chain of command would show some compassion and allow him to leave the Falklands. They hadn't yet announced their engagement or requested permission to marry so the Army could keep him there. There would be absolutely no point because, as Major Best knew full well, Corporal Warbutton would be absolutely no good to man nor beast while the woman he loved hovered between life and death.

Mouse left Rheindahlen at two o'clock. By the time she found her way to her accommodation, it was almost nine. They had been allocated first floor flats just around the corner from the camp in an area that housed both military and German civilian personnel. She was told they were both two bedroom flats and hers was directly opposite where Grace's parents would stay. Mouse couldn't wait until the next day to see Grace. Extremely upset and worried about her close friend, it had been a struggle for her to concentrate on the long drive to Celle. The duty driver had been detailed to take her to the hospital. Grace had been stabilised then moved to Hannover Krankenhaus, a hospital that specialised in spinal injuries. The driver gave up trying to chat after a few minutes and Mouse spent the journey staring out of the window. The reception staff spoke excellent English – the hospital had received many British forces patients in the past – and directed Mouse to the intensive care unit. Grace was alone in a small room. She seemed tiny amongst all the machines and wires that were hooked up to various parts of her body. Mouse's hand involuntary flew to her mouth as she took in the scene; it all seemed so unreal. Grace with her gentle elegance and calming influence lying motionless on the bed, fighting for her life. Hans, who introduced himself as the male nurse, noticed her distress and putting an arm around her, steered Mouse into the room. Although she'd never seen a dead body, looking at her friend and future sister-in-law, Mouse imagined this was how one would look. Grace's long brown hair had turned grey – Hans told her that this was due to the shock of the accident. Her face was an unhealthy pallor made worse by the almost purple lines under her eyes. Mouse doubted she would recover.

Seeing her distress, Hans guided her to the seat next to Grace's bed.

'She has suffered much trauma.' His dulcet tones belied the seriousness of the situation. 'She will be kept in a coma until the doctor says she can be woken. That's when the hard work will begin,' he squeezed her shoulder. 'She will need all the love and support then. It is a long, hard journey.'

'So she will definitely wake up then?'

'I cannot say. I am only a male nurse.'

Mouse burst into tears and Hans handed her a tissue. 'Talk to your friend. Some believe that people in comas can hear. If you can, play her the music she likes. Tell her funny stories, or remind her of good times. Give her plenty of reasons to wake up.'

126

'I've brought a cassette player with her favourite music. I thought she might like it.' Mouse removed the player from her rucksack and started sorting through the cassettes.

'That's a good idea, but it's too late now. We'll put the music on tomorrow. I'll leave you for a while.'

Sitting next to Grace she held her hand.

'Go on. Talk to her,' said Hans, the male nurse as she now thought of him because of the amount of times he'd said it. She waited until he left the room before speaking to Grace. 'I've brought you Madness, and Survivor and, in case you fancy dancing, Donna Summer.' She wondered if she should have joked about dancing under the circumstances. 'I hope I don't get a bollocking for that when you wake up.' She laughed nervously, feeling a bit stupid talking to Grace when she didn't know if her words could be heard. She carried on anyway. 'We've sent Graham's unit a signal, he should be granted compassionate leave so will be back to see you within a few days. Your Mum and Dad are flying in to Hannover tomorrow by the way. I'm dying to meet them. I might as well tell you what happened when me and Guy were on leave.' Now in full swing and with a captive audience, Mouse found it hard to shut up. Hans returned thirty minutes later.

'You should go now and get some sleep.'

'I don't want to leave her all on her own. What if...'

'She's not on her own. We're here all night you know and Grace is in a stable condition Please, go and get some sleep. It is going to be difficult for her parents tomorrow, they may need your strength.'

Mouse admitted reluctantly that Hans was right. Grace's parents would be very distressed so she had to be strong for them. She gave her hand a squeeze and said goodnight before going in search of the driver who was smoking a cigarette outside his car.

'How is she?'

Mouse shook her head sadly. She knew she wasn't very good company at the moment but made an effort on the return journey – it couldn't be much fun for the driver, ferrying people around who couldn't even be bothered to talk to him.

*****

Grace watched as three horses galloped by. Two had babies on their backs, the third had already thrown the baby and the infant was still alive, screaming its heart out. Grace screamed at the horses to stop but they took no notice. She was exhausted and her throat was red raw, but still they kept on galloping.

She dangled her hand in a stream and looked at her reflection in the water. The wind blew her hair away from her face and the skirt of her white long-sleeved nightie billowed around her. She wanted to dip her toes in the water but when she tried to move her legs, nothing happened. She heard a horse whinny in the distance and stood up to look in the direction of the noise. Five were galloping towards her this time, each had a baby in the saddle and the infants were being bounced around. Grace looked on in horror as one by one the babies were thrown out of their saddles and into the air. She screamed as one headed toward the stream. The baby smiled at her as it flew past.

*****

Grace's parents and Elaine arrived the following day. Mouse still didn't know whether Graham would be allowed to leave the Falklands, but if he was, there was a room with a bed in the apartment that she shared with Elaine. They were all in shock. Grace had always been the one to offer comfort to others in times of distress so it was hard to see her lying there, at death's door. Mouse was convinced that Graham's presence, along with that of her parents, would give Grace all the fight she needed to increase her chances of recovery. Her mother offered comfort to Mouse and Elaine, and thanked every member of staff that she met. Mouse was amazed at her kindness and strength of character, now knowing whom Grace took after. Her father was a gentle giant, quiet but with a presence that drew stares when he walked into a room.

They took turns sitting with her and talking. It was on the fourth day, two hours after Graham's arrival that her eyes flickered. She opened them a little while later and smiled when she saw her parents, Graham, Mouse and Elaine. Her eyes lingered on Graham. Grace looked at peace, until she attempted to move and then the distress showed clearly on her face. Her mother stroked her hair and soothed her as if she were a little girl, but all Mouse remembered was how confused and upset she'd looked before going back to sleep. The doctors had already told her mother and father that Grace's back trauma was so bad it was unlikely she would ever walk again. They'd agreed that her parents would give her the news, when she woke, but only when the medical staff

128

believed she was strong enough to hear it. Graham would be present to offer love and support.

*****

The situation with Mouse was driving Guy mad. He'd had time to think and had to admit he'd been a bit of a bastard to Elaine, so was willing to back down on that one. If they cut her in half he was sure they'd find *Army* written inside her, so deep down he now knew she wouldn't do anything to compromise her career, or anyone else's. He'd speak to Elaine first then tell Mouse his decision. They were both still with Grace. Guy had been glad to hear from Mouse, even briefly when she contacted him to tell him that Grace had woken. He still didn't know how they were going to overcome their differences about Mouse's career but hearing her voice again for the first time in weeks made him absolutely certain he wanted her in his life for good. If that meant compromise, so be it, but if he was willing to, she had to give a bit too. He'd have to wait until they were together to talk about it. It was too delicate to discuss on the phone. In the meantime he'd need to focus on the next few weeks if he wanted to embark on a new chapter of his Army career.

He shared the mini-bus with five others, one of them female. Guy assumed they'd all received the same instructions as they introduced themselves by first name only and gave nothing away about their personal histories. He hadn't been to this area before and they noticed the usual *MOD PROPERTY – KEEP OUT* sign, and warning to trespassers as they reached the camp. There was a perimeter fence but no buildings were visible as the driver drove slowly down the uneven track. After a few minutes they came to a barrier which was manned by a civilian Ministry of Defence Guard. He checked and double-checked their ID cards and chatted to the driver – it was obvious they knew each other. They were given the go ahead and the driver followed the signs for reception and parked up. Guy counted eight cars in the car park. The driver turned to his passengers. 'Right, boys and girl. This is where we part company. Grab your kit, someone will meet you shortly.'

They watched with some trepidation as he drove off, and looked at their surroundings. There were a number of old buildings in various states of disrepair, some fields further away with another two buildings behind them that looked in a better condition from this distance. A number of four-ton trucks and mini-buses were parked next to the two buildings. On the other side of the vehicles were four longer buildings that looked like accommodation blocks. Lights were on in two. Guy assumed that the building standing alongside the accommodation blocks was the cookhouse.

A man approached the car park. He was wearing military lightweights, a plain green belt, boots and t-shirt. Nothing on his uniform indicated his rank or regimental affiliation, which was very unusual for forces personnel. He was wiry and looked fit, but unremarkable.

'Pick up your kit and follow me. Do exactly as you're told and address all instructors as staff.'

'Yes, staff,' they said in unison, instantly taken back to their days of basic training. By the time they'd picked up their gear, the instructor had jogged away. He turned to face them, running backwards as he did so. 'Come on you lot, keep up!' They moved into action, uncomfortable with various items jangling in their pockets, but trying their best to catch up.

As they arrived at the building with lights on they were told to drop their kit, face the wall and not to move or talk until instructed to do so. Guy had noticed three other blokes already standing, facing the wall. After what seemed like an age, an instructor came and tapped the bloke next to him on the shoulder. The girl and two of the other blokes he'd travelled with had already left and Guy was starting to feel paranoid. He couldn't be sure but it seemed at least another five minutes before he received his tap on the shoulder and instructions. Following them to the letter, he entered the building and knocked on the first door on the right. Told to go in, he was given a two-digit number, which he had to hold up while the man he assumed was the clerk took his photograph. After the photograph he was issued with a badge, but instead of having his name, it had the number seventy-five. He was told that he'd be known as seventy-five for the duration of the course, or for as long as he lasted. 'Always wear that badge on your chest, left-hand side and do not reveal your identity, unit or history to anyone while you are here,' said a female instructor. Guy was bemused that females were permitted into this environment, but not into the regular special forces. 'Yes, staff,' he answered.

He was told to put his keys, ID card and wallet into a tray, which was secured in a safe in his presence. 'They'll be returned to you on your departure. Now get your bags and follow me.' Guy did as bid and they eventually arrived at the accommodation. He was in a twelve-man room and eight of the bed spaces had already been taken, including those next to the windows. Guy chose the bed furthest from the door and put his bags down next to it. He unfolded the starched sheets and cream hairy blankets and set about making his bed, covering it with the bright green counterpane once he'd finished. He checked out the ablutions across the corridor when an instructor appeared and told them all to get into boots and lightweights and report to what they called the test room, as soon as possible.

They were instructed to write about themselves on four sides of paper. After thirty minutes they were told to stop. Guy looked up. He guessed there were at least eighty others in the room now, some of whom had arrived while he had been writing. A man walked to the front of the room and all their eyes followed his movements. Like the other instructors, he didn't wear any rank, but Guy could tell from the body language of those around him that he was the boss.

'We demand very high standards that most of you will fail to meet.' He looked around as if checking who would succeed. 'Try your very best at all times and if you fail, remember that it's not personal. If it gets too much for you, you can leave at any time. Good luck.'

He left as quickly as he'd arrived and one of the other instructors took over, telling them all to change into PT kit and to place what they'd written into the burn bag at the front of the room. Chaos ensued as they all rushed towards the burn bag and then the exit, hoping to be the first to impress their instructor.

The following day set the tempo. As soon as they'd finished one task they were rushed to the next. PT sessions, IQ tests, psychological evaluations and mind games. They were put into dark rooms where they had to find their way out while blindfolded, and identify objects by touch alone. Then into rooms containing a number of objects and people where they would be required to identify the contents and the programme that was playing on the TV, later on back in the test room. Guy wasn't sure whether he preferred the mental or physical tests. When he'd arrived he was confident that he was fitter than he'd ever been, and probably a lot fitter than the others who would attend the course. Now he wasn't sure. The mental stress coupled with physical exertion meant that this was one of the toughest courses any of them would ever experience. Guy was tired to his very core. The only consolation was that everyone else felt exactly the same. He'd completed the hardest week of his life and instead of wanting to throw in the towel, he was even more determined to succeed. Lack of sleep, physical exertion and not knowing what was coming next put the trainees on edge. Looking around as they attended another lecture, he counted thirty-six others and wondered briefly how many would be left by the end. He quickly snapped his brain back to attention and waited to discover what the next challenge would bring.

The evening was spent in tatty civilian clothing with three other trainees, doing a recce inside a rough public house. They had to memorise as much information of the pub's interior as possible, without the locals discovering what they were doing. On return to the base they were required to make plans of the pub – both inside and out – and the local area. Despite believing that his group had done quite well, they were ripped to shreds by the instructors. One of the four had reached the end of his tether. Pushing his chair back he stood up. 'I'm out,' he said, and then quietly left the room. The instructors didn't react. The trainees had been told they could leave at any time.

They crashed into bed after two in the morning and were woken at five thirty by a cheery instructor who told them to get into running kit. After a hard session followed by breakfast, more tests followed. The tempo didn't change and one by one, their number reduced. For the final task they were told to dress in casual civilian clothing and to bring a small rucksack, but no cash. It was difficult to know what to take so they packed enough for overnight. Their bags and person were checked before they were instructed to get onto a bus and money and compasses were removed. The windows of the bus were blacked out and the trainees were all blindfolded. They were allocated a partner and dropped off in their pairs at different locations. Each pair was given a different list of items and told to report back to base by midday the following day, with a bag containing all the items on the list. It was pitch black and Guy and his partner, forty-eight, were at the edge of a field in what appeared to be the middle of nowhere. They agreed on the names they would call each other for the duration of the exercise. Guy used his small torch to scan the items on the list. Some of them would be easier to obtain than others but as they read, they both knew they'd have to use guile and initiative to get hold of a hairbrush, used bus ticket, library book, sandwich, a garage key and a red rose.

'Especially as we don't have any cash,' said Guy.

His partner smirked, sat on the grass and removed his right boot. He wacked the heel of the boot on the ground and part of it appeared to come loose. Guy was intrigued as a piece of rolled up paper dropped out. He handed the paper to Guy and pushed the heel hard with one hand and the boot with the other. The heel clicked back into place. Guy unrolled the paper and laughed. He gave his partner a manly punch in the arm and handed him the ten-pound note, thankful that one of them had shown such initiative. They walked for three hours until they came to the outskirts of a village. Checking out the name they now knew how far they were from the camp. They decided to find a farm with a barn they could sleep in, then make their way to the village at first light. The items could be bought or procured by other means, and if they were careful, they'd have enough left to catch a bus to a few miles from the camp.

Back at the camp Guy and the remaining seventeen were tired, but happy that it was almost over. There was nothing more they could do and were split into two groups, eleven in one and six others in the group with Guy. The eleven were called to attention by an instructor and told to follow him. Guy and the others - one of them forty-eight, his partner from the previous night's exercise - waited anxiously as the chief instructor stood in front of them.

'Well done. You've passed the first part of selection. The next stage is further basic training for a very specialised role in Northern Ireland. The small number that pass will move on to advanced training. Security is paramount and you are to keep any personal details to yourself. The only person authorised to know your real identity and parent unit, is the chief clerk. We will inform your commanding officers of your future movements. Your belongings will be boxed up and sent to your new location if you pass the course. I suggest you tell your families, lovers and close friends that you are on an adventure training course for the next month or so. Further details will follow for those lucky few,' he grinned and looked around, 'who manage to pass the next phase.'

They were informed that they were to have two weeks leave and were then to report to a certain railway station by three o'clock, on the final Monday of their leave. 'You will be taken to our training camp at a secret location. For obvious reasons we work on a strictly need to know basis so this information should not be discussed with anyone. During your training you will be known by your own first name or a name of your choosing. You decide which. Make the most of your leave, it may be your last for quite some time.'

They were told to report to the Orderly Room for final administration before departure, and then went their separate ways to enjoy a well-earned rest.

*****

Graham had been granted two weeks leave. He'd been told he wasn't returning to the Falkland Islands and was to report back to his Squadron once his leave was over. His OC was a decent guy and he knew he could chance pushing it to three weeks if he needed to – and the way things were going, he just might. Within forty-eight hours of returning to consciousness, Grace had told him she didn't want to be with him any more and that he deserved a *full woman*. She'd been through such a traumatic experience all he'd wanted to do was to hold her, comfort her and let her know how much he loved her. She was having none of it. Frustration had made him leave her bedside to find a quiet space and count to a couple of hundred before returning. Graham hadn't before realised quite how stubborn Grace could be. His sister and Elaine quickly put him in the picture, and leaving the room to scream or swear at the invisible god of fate became his norm. Moving from *denial* to an *I'll show them* phase, Grace had quickly progressed to a wheelchair. Although the medics were impressed by her sheer will and stubborn determination, they wanted to keep it real and none were willing to tell her that occasionally, miracles did happen. Grace was grumpy and unpredictable so required handling with care. It was during this period that Colonel Jacobson, the senior British WRAC officer came to visit. The colonel was used to being the centre of attention and had a habit of engaging her tongue before her brain.

'Thanks for coming, ma'am.' Grace smiled at the senior officer.

The colonel leaned on the bed and took hold of Grace's right hand. She smiled benevolently, hoping that the other visitors were looking. 'I know you're very active, Corporal Fleming,' she patted her hand. 'You'll be able to play wheelchair basketball and I've heard it's very competitive.'

Grace believed she would walk again and her mood changed from being grateful to hateful. She withdrew her hand as if about to be attacked by a striking snake. For the first time, she took a proper look at the middle-aged woman sitting on the chair next to her bed. Dyed blonde hair, too much make-up and a chest fighting to get out of her lovat green jumper, she realised that Colonel Jacobson was visiting to satisfy her own needs, not to help or encourage her. She couldn't believe what she'd just heard and for the first time in her adult life acted on impulse rather than intelligence. She listened to her own voice, as if viewing the scene from another dimension.

'Get out!'

Nobody had ever spoken to the colonel like that and she stared at Grace, before finding her voice. 'But, Corporal Fleming that's totally uncalled for. I've given up my time...'

Without hesitation, Grace picked up the bedpan. By the time Colonel Jacobson realised what was happening it was too late. 'You will pay for this, young lady!'

Grace laughed like a lunatic as her visitor tried to stop the urine dripping from her hair onto the shiny badges of rank on her shoulder. Trying to keep her composure, Colonel Jacobson shook her head and walked from the ward, head held high, reminding Grace of Miss Piggy from the Muppet Show.

She assumed she wouldn't be a lance corporal for much longer. She couldn't walk so wasn't particularly bothered about having a stripe on her arm for the limited time she had left in the Army.

The release that the temper tantrum had given her seemed to focus Grace. She wasn't any happier with her situation but suddenly became aware of other people's feelings, as well as her own. She noticed the hangdog expression on Graham's face every time she responded negatively to his optimism. Gradually, she began to believe that he did actually love her for who she was, rather than only seeing the cripple she'd become. She still held on to a belief that he could do better but her determination to get rid of him waned every day. She wasn't yet ready to tell him directly, but Graham noticed the changes.

Mrs Fleming had been outraged at the insensitive comments made by Colonel Jacobson. She said nothing to the others but wrote to the Commander in Chief, British Army of the Rhine to express her disgust. The general was relieved that she hadn't written to her MP or *The Sun* newspaper, and there was no way that Lance Corporal Fleming was going to lose her stripe due to insubordination. She would be medically discharged as a lance corporal, not as a private soldier. Colonel Jacobson wasn't impressed, but accepted she'd been insensitive, so didn't force the issue. She knew which side her bread was buttered and no way would she go up against her handsome Commander-in-Chief – unless it was a physical going up against and that was a different matter entirely.

*****

Grace was out of immediate danger but had changed so much since the accident that it was like being with a different person at times. Graham loved her and was still determined to be with her, especially now her protestations that she no longer loved him and they would be better off without each other became less frequent. He was trying to get detached to a unit in Germany so he could be nearer during her rehabilitation. Grace would eventually move back to the UK but as the Hannover hospital had state of the art facilities for those who'd suffered back injuries, it was agreed she would remain there for a while longer. The exact timeframe was unspecified and would depend on the progress she made. Graham's chain of command already knew he planned to marry Grace so they requested that his Records Office in Hastings detach him to a unit in Germany, allowing him to be near his fiancée during this crucial time. He hadn't told anyone in authority that, at the moment, Grace was lukewarm to his advances. Her father had his own business and had left his partner in charge. He would pop back to the UK occasionally but Grace's mother was happy to remain in Germany, knowing that her daughter was receiving the best medical support possible. They were fairly well off so money wasn't a major issue. They were happy to pay the going rent for the flat but the Signals unit declined. The specialist had told Mr and Mrs Fleming that personality changes were a common occurrence after suffering such trauma and that many patients eventually returned to normal. He was unwilling to make any predications in Grace's case and had advised them to give it time. To everyone that loved her, it seemed the answer to every question was to *give it time.*

The situation with Grace had made Mouse realise just how fragile life was. Despite the worry about her friend, she was determined to enjoy her time with Guy before he was off again attempting to achieve what she thought impossible for most. Knowing him, he would pass and then put himself in danger somewhere in Northern Ireland. She was torn between wanting to know exactly what he'd be doing and wanting to bury her head in the sand. Whatever happened, she was determined they'd enjoy their time together.

This would be the last time he could relax before having to face God only knew what and as much as she wanted to, she didn't have it in her to push him for answers. They'd made love for the final time and as he nodded off, Mouse held him and revelled in his warmth. She ran her hand along the hair on his chin, still trying to get used to the idea of her man with a beard, and smiling to herself as she recalled it tickling some intimate places earlier. Mouse nuzzled into his chest taking in the smell and feel of him, trying to embed it onto her brain to make a permanent memory of this moment, just in case...

Guy kissed the top of her head and mumbled a few words, incoherent in his sleep. He turned and Mouse turned with him. As he spooned her she drifted off to sleep, content in their cocoon of love.

Over a leisurely breakfast at the hotel, Mouse tried to make light of the situation. 'So you're going on adventurous training for a month, coz all of a sudden your unit is now up to full manning?' she asked.

'Yup, that's about it.'

'And bears don't shit in the woods.'

Guy shook his head and laughed. She was sometimes gullible but she wasn't stupid. They both knew what he was up to but there was no way he would discuss it openly.

'Good luck with it, Guy. Although I wish you every success with your *adventure training*,' she raised her eyebrows. 'A small part of me hopes that you fail. Is that completely selfish?'

He understood. She'd obviously done her homework and knew he could be in danger if he followed this particular career path, though neither of them yet knew the extent of that danger. 'Come here.'

She entered his embrace and he held her for a moment, both deep in their own thoughts.

'Will you stand by me, Mouse?'

She lifted her head. 'Is it what you really want?'

'Definitely.'

'Then I'm behind you one hundred per cent. Good luck, Guy.' She meant it this time and watched as he departed, knowing he was apprehensive, but ready to take on the next phase of his training.

*****

Guy was directed to a mini-bus and was soon joined by eight others. They chatted about nothing in particular, all wary of sharing any personal information. They arrived after a three- hour drive. The camp was out in the sticks, not visible from any of the local roads. They were shown around the small cluster of buildings comprising a small cookhouse, accommodation blocks, bar and TV room, lecture facility and classrooms. Guy could see that he wasn't the only one to be pleasantly surprised by the spacious and modern four-man rooms. The training area was pointed out to them, together with a man made vehicle course. The perimeter fence in the distance was topped with barbed wire. MOD police with guard dogs patrolled the area and cameras were dotted around. It was obvious that security was taken very seriously. As more personnel arrived, they were right to assume that the camp was for the exclusive use of the trainees, their instructors and support staff.

The trainees who had passed the two-week selection course during the previous four months, reported to the lecture facility for a briefing from the chief instructor. They were all dressed in casual civilian clothes, as were all the instructors. The chief, a powerful looking man, explained they would work to the max for the next three months and any failures would be out. They were to concentrate on the skills being taught and were expected to master them before some, but not all, would be given the opportunity to move on. The first was advanced driving, not the type taught to sensible, experienced drivers, but techniques that would enable them to make a hasty withdrawal from life or death situations. Guy crawled into his bed that night, exhausted after a long day learning new driving techniques followed by the usual tough PT session, then after supper, lectures and instruction on vehicle recognition. His brain was buzzing despite its weariness, and that of his body.

There were four girls on the course, one, Jackie, had accompanied him, Paul and the instructor in the car that day. Guy and Paul had joked about women drivers but Jackie let her driving do the talking. They were amazed at how quickly she picked up the new techniques. Guy and Paul held on for dear life as she executed a perfect overtake through a tight bend, reassuring them that she was able to read the road ahead. Guy developed a grudging respect for her and wished he could drive as well as she had. After stopping as instructed she turned to them. 'What was that about women drivers, fellas?' They all laughed and for Guy at least, it relieved the tension of some of her more daring manoeuvres.

Their course instructors were both male and female. One of the women, he was told, was the most skilled driver of them all. He had to accept that they were all in the same boat and all of the instructors had passed the tough course and carried out duties that he could only imagine, regardless of their gender. Women could not serve with the special forces but the British public were being duped if they thought all members of the WRAC were non-combatant! Guy knew that Mouse wouldn't be into this type of training, her talents lay elsewhere, but he also knew he had to accept that some women were as tough as men – a complete change to his previous attitude.

The programme was packed and physical training followed the daily driving lessons and car maintenance activities. No matter how hard they tried, none of the trainees could keep up with any of the instructors. Lectures usually took place after supper. The topics were wide and varied including signals voice procedures, first aid, further vehicle recognition techniques and intelligence information about weapons that potential enemies were likely to use.

More of the same followed and those who passed the high-speed advanced driving test two weeks later, were progressed to the next phase. Like everything else on the course the test was tough and Guy drove the Ford Escort to his and the vehicle's limits. Relief was the main emotion he felt when given the news that he'd passed. Those that didn't meet the exacting standards packed their bags and departed.

Those that remained were briefed about what was to follow. They were introduced to a Royal Army Ordnance Corps photographer, Angus. He looked to be in his mid-thirties and sported a moustache, which had more hair than his shiny, bald head. He told them he would teach them everything they needed to know about photography during their time together.

'But first, you're going to need one of these.' He showed them a basic Nikon camera and his assistant gave everyone a bag containing the same camera and all the other kit they would need.

Over the next days and weeks they learnt about film speeds, depth preview, focal length, f-stops and apertures. Lenses and which to use, lighting, shutter-speeds, photographing moving objects and taking photographs at night were also covered in great depth. Although it was unlikely they'd be required to process their own films while working as operators, they had to learn how do so and spent time developing the negatives into black and white prints. Like many of his colleagues, Guy had little interest in photography to start with, but soon realised that the ability to take decent photographs of suspects could prove invaluable to other operators, as well as the Army's Intelligence Corps. He applied himself to the techniques and it wasn't long before he was totally absorbed in his duties. Towards the end of the second week, Guy was able to confidently take photographs in total darkness, outside and in, and produce prints that were sharp enough to distinguish the details.

The complexity of aerial photography came next where the trainees were required to take shots from Lynx and Gazelle helicopters, and then present the results for inspection by both Angus and the other instructors. Video camera techniques followed and after the basics, they had to learn how to operate cameras that were hidden in briefcases or handbags.

Following the practical tests in all aspects of photography, numbers were whittled down yet again. Despite their intelligence and skills in other areas, Paul and Jackie were two of the casualties at this stage.

Guy was excited about the next phase of training, surveillance. He'd already covered some basic surveillance techniques during his military police training for the Army's Special Investigation Branch. He watched and listened intently, knowing that he still had lots to learn. The first lecture covered a basic follow with details of code names for the main target, his vehicle and home address or main location. Further lectures covered proper use of radio systems, including how to wear them discreetly on their bodies and conceal the microphones, as demonstrated by their instructor. They were also taught how to speak without moving their lips, as if they were ventriloquists. Guy found it difficult to master making contradictory head and hand movements while talking – a requirement so that alert observers wouldn't notice them speaking. They also learnt about the particular radio language operators used, about stakeout options, the positioning of individual members of the surveillance team and the difference between carrying out a job on the mainland and in Northern Ireland. It was the job of customs, MI5 or the police to carry out surveillance on the mainland and the public would usually ignore an unmarked car. It was different in a typically republican or loyalist area in Northern Ireland where the occupants of such a vehicle were likely be challenged. The population were always on their guard due to the suffering a large number had endured and sectarian murders that had affected many. It made sense and brought home the fact that if they passed the course, the new operators would be in serious situations that required them to put their lives at risk on a daily basis.

After three months of intensive training, the trainees were given a weekend off to recharge their batteries. Mouse was on exercise so they weren't able to see each other. Guy decided to take the time to visit his family and was glad to see that Mrs Jarvis and Mr Barston still enjoyed each other's company, but more importantly for his own peace of mind, cared deeply for his siblings and provided a stable influence in their lives. He returned to the secret location, full of enthusiasm for the next stage of his training but oblivious to the surprise that awaited him.

*****

Mouse slung her heavy rucksack onto her back and boarded the transport. The hard green seats on the long white bus were marginally more comfortable than the benches in the back of a four-tonner, and for that she was grateful. She was tired from the long hours on exercise and in need of a shower. What made her most grumpy was that she'd missed Guy by only one week. He'd had no say in when he could have time off and she'd had to go on exercise. *Ours is not to reason why...* she thought. Even though she had no choice, it didn't make her feel any happier knowing that she wouldn't see him for God only knew how long. She'd have to suck it up and get on with her life until then, despite aching for him daily.

Feeling more human after a long shower and good night's sleep, Mouse decided she needed cheering up. She decided to go to her aerobics class and then have a few drinks and some fun during the weekend. Returning from her class she was about to knock on Spike's door when she heard footsteps along the corridor. Her natural curiosity got the better of her and as she turned to look, her jaw almost hit the floor.

'What the...'

Moira Jones frowned when she saw Mouse.

'What are you doing here?' asked Mouse.

Spike opened her door. 'Ah, I see you know. *Corporal* Jones lives in Block B.' Block B was next door to where Mouse and Spike were accommodated.

'What do you mean Corporal Jones? I thought...'

'She's a full screw now,' Spike whispered so Moira Jones couldn't hear.

'I hear you're a full-screw now, Warbutton,' Moira had found her tongue. 'They must be giving them away these days.'

'Obviously not if you're back to corporal, Jones. You'll keep out of my effing way if you know what's good for you.' She pushed Spike into her room and followed her in, quickly shutting the door behind them.

Moira Jones stood looking at the door for a few seconds, totally humiliated that one of the former junior NCOs who she happened to despise, was now of equal rank, despite her part in orchestrating her demotion to private. She didn't plan on publicising the fact that Warbutton had been done for beating her up; that would make her look feeble. Thoughts of that night came flooding back and Moira struggled to keep control. She'd already done a bit of digging and discovered that Warbutton's ex, a Lance Corporal called KC Cooke, who she'd apparently jilted at the altar, was based in Monchengladbach. If that rumour were true he probably hated Warbutton as much as she did. Moira made a silent vow to teach the girly clerk a lesson and started to form a plan.

Before Mouse had a chance to gather her thoughts, Spike started chattering. 'That was fucking awesome! You showed her. I wanted to let you know before you bumped into her but thought you'd be having a lie-in after coming back from exercise...'

'Why isn't she a sergeant? I wonder if...' Before Mouse could voice her concerns about whether Guy had anything to do with the demotion after promising not to, Spike interrupted.

'Apparently she couldn't pass her education. I heard her OC thought she was OK and was going to fight her corner, but one of her girls complained to her sergeant major that she was picking on her. That was enough for the decision to be made and here she is, Corporal Jones.' Spike giggled and Mouse joined in. So she'd had her comeuppance and Guy had absolutely nothing to do with it. There was such a thing as karma after all.

142

'Fancy the Marley tonight,' Mouse asked, once they'd both calmed down. They made the arrangements and she returned to her bunk to think about the situation. Already knowing what Moira Jones was really like, she realised that the woman would be out to get her. Despite her initial euphoria about her demotion, it didn't give Mouse any comfort knowing that she now had two enemies at large, both of whom she would need to avoid at all costs.

*****

Although he knew along with everyone else that the rest of the course would be hard work, he also knew that his chances of success increased with every passing day. They'd spent the last week recapping their training and had taken part in exercises where they'd had to follow suspects in various different scenarios; taking photographs without being discovered. The final part of the exercise had been to report their findings back to the instructors where their shortcomings were pointed out. This was the only way they could improve and learn from their mistakes, which became less frequent as they gained experience.

They were called to the lecture theatre for a briefing. The chief instructor stood in front of the rostrum. 'Well done ladies and gents for making it to this phase. Don't rest on your laurels. You still have a lot to learn. Now you're going to be teamed up with experienced operators for the next part of your training. Watch, listen and learn. These people have been there and done it. Any questions?' he paused and there was silence. 'When your name is called, go to the location as instructed and you'll be told who will be holding your hand.'

Guy's was the last name and he was to be paired with a woman. He'd long since got over his hang-ups about women being weaker and was looking forward to meeting her. Gaynor. He made his way to the building he'd been told to report to and didn't even attempt to hide his surprise when he saw her.

'Hi, Guy. How's it going.'

'What the?' Memories came flooding back of their intimate relationship in the days before he'd fallen in love with Mouse. He laughed and put out his hand for her to shake. Gaynor moved in for a hug but Guy put an arm around her and clapped her back in a blokey embrace, hoping to set the boundaries straight away. She raised her eyebrows and a smile played around her lips.

'Someone's got a sense or humour. I've been selected to mentor you and I'll be reporting back to the instructors.' Expecting a reaction, she was surprised when he didn't respond. The Guy Halfpenny she knew would struggle to take direction from a woman. 'If you have a problem with that, I need to know about it now.'

'You've passed the course?'

'Yup.'

'Done a stint as an operator?'

'Two tours, yeah.'

'Then no problem. I want this and I'm eager to learn.'

Now it was Gaynor's turn to hide her surprise. 'Right, let's get on. We have a surveillance job to do at an O.P. Bring your camera gear, and everything you think you'll need for some time in the woods. We depart in ten minutes.'

Just as he thought the training might be less knackering, they'd actually increased the tempo. Guy rushed to his accommodation and packed his kit, carefully at first. He'd packed too many clothes and was unable to fit in the camera accessories. He gave himself a reality check and repacked quickly, remembering the minimal amount of kit the instructors had displayed when they taught them about covert observation posts – OPs.

They were dropped off in the woods and had to make their way to the outskirts of a farm without being seen. They'd already had the opportunity to put their training into practise on a few occasions, setting up their own OPs in bushes and hedgerows, while learning from the instructors who were able to blend perfectly into their surroundings.

A thorough recce of the farm building established that nobody was home.

'Find a suitable O.P location,' said Gaynor. 'You know what to look for?' Guy said yes and set about the task. She discounted the first two locations that he thought suitable but agreed with his third, a bush. Guy pulled back the foliage carefully and constructed a tunnel small enough for one person to crawl through at a time. He made two separate holes for their kit and ensured there was enough room for them both to lie down and to make small movements. After sorting the roof, Gaynor gave it the once over. His OP was good but with a few adjustments she made it even better. As it started to get dark they were left with a perfectly camouflaged OP with a small opening, big enough for the camera lens to point through. From his training, Guy knew that the few small ferns hanging down in front of the lens would not affect the quality of the photographs, as long as they took this into consideration while taking shots.

The next forty-eight hours consisted of one sleeping while the other was on watch, recording everything that happened in or around the building. At least Guy was sleeping when he wasn't on duty. He wondered if Gaynor was actually sleeping, or whether she was monitoring his progress, even though her eyes were closed. They were required to perform hourly radio checks and to eat and drink cold rations. Both had been issued bottles to urinate into and freezer bags for defecation. By the time the radio call came to tell them to pack up, Guy was relieved to be able to crawl backwards out of the OP and even more relieved that he hadn't needed to crap while holed up with Gaynor.

He was shattered and so were all the other teams. Muscles were stiff and aching from lack of movement and bodies were tired from lack of decent sleep and proper meals. After a meal and showers all round, they were told to parade outside in their PT kit and boots. The instructors ran them hard, all the way to the assault course. The operators who they'd teamed up with were the only ones not surprised at being told to complete the course as quickly as they could. They were lined up and set off at thirty second intervals – the trainees were told their mission was to beat the time of their partner. Despite his new respect for women, Guy was still seething when he discovered that Gaynor's time was eight seconds faster than his. None of the trainees had been able to beat their partner's time, but this was of little consolation to Guy.

As the training continued, Guy wondered how Mouse would feel if she discovered he was to be permanently partnered with a woman he had been intimate with before they met. He wouldn't be happy if she spent so much time with an ex, even though he knew how much she loved him. Despite being entirely professional Guy sensed that Gaynor still held a candle for him. If his instincts were correct he knew this could be a problem. He stopped ruminating and put all thoughts of Mouse out of his head for the time being. He had work to do and needed to give it his full concentration if he hoped to shorten the career of a number of terrorists in the future.

They'd had their briefing and had been given details of their tasks. It was Friday evening. Guy and Gaynor had to integrate with some people in a bar, and obtain the driving licence or passport details of a woman, together with her date of birth, and the address of a man. They had to do this without causing any suspicion or aggro. In the car on the way to the town they discussed tactics and agreed it would be better to pose as a couple.

'We can pretend we're away for a romantic weekend,' said Gaynor, 'people trust a couple more than a single man or woman.'

'You'd love that wouldn't you,' muttered Guy. He stopped at the red light and looked at her.

'Don't flatter yourself. You know the score. If you have a problem with it you only have to say.'

He would have preferred a different partner but wasn't going to rock the boat, especially as he could be thrown out of it at any time.

'It's fine.'

'Well stop having a go then. Let's just do the job.'

It was ironic that they were already arguing like an old couple, but she was right. 'Fair enough. But it's purely professional.'

'Got it.' Although Gaynor had said otherwise, she was still hoping for the opportunity to change his mind. They'd be in stressful situations during their work together so she was prepared to be patient.

The intensive training continued and the days merged into weeks. At the start of their final two weeks the experienced operators left. Following the capture and interrogation exercise in which the special forces had assisted to make it as realistic as possible, a number of trainees broke down and were removed from the course. Some further work on urban operations followed, then the final exercise where they were required to carry out the full remit of an operator, in a realistic situation. For this they were split into teams and were to work within a tough council estate amongst civilians. Mistakes would mean being discovered by unfriendly members of the local civilian population. Guy knew he couldn't have worked any harder and by the time the course ended, was satisfied that he'd done everything he could to pass. As they sat in the lecture theatre they all waited as the chief instructor made his way to the rostrum to let them know their fate.

Out of the twenty-eight who had come this far, Guy was one of twenty-one who had passed. He was elated and looking forward to some time off before his deployment to Northern Ireland.

*****

'So obviously you're going to be undercover, but what's the score?' asked Mouse.

'Meaning what, exactly?' Guy had shaved off his beard. As he twirled his moustache Mouse laughed, thinking he looked like a character out of a spaghetti western. She forced herself to regain control. This was serious. 'Meaning how many are in your team? Who are you going to be working with? The SAS?'

Since the Iranian Embassy Siege a few years before, the SAS had been elevated to superhero status by members of the British public. It irritated Guy that Mouse spoke with the same awe when she mentioned them. Although he was not SAS he was now a member of the special forces. Mouse had no idea that this was the case or that Guy was in receipt of the extra pay that went with the honour of being a member of that very small club.

'I could tell you, but I'd have to shoot you.'

'Yeah, yeah,' she laughed. 'But seriously? You know I'll only worry about you if I don't know what's going on.'

Guy hesitated. There was no way he could tell her he would be working with Gaynor if he wanted his testicles to remain intact.

'We'll be working in small teams to gather information and quite possibly infiltrate terrorist cells. We'll have to build relationships with the locals to get them to trust us.'

'Relationships?' Mouse frowned. 'Does that include relationships with women.'

'No, Mouse,' he sighed. 'There may be a chance that some women soldiers will also come with us, so it could look as if we are already with someone if you know what I mean.' He wasn't exactly lying to her but wasn't telling her the full truth either. He could see that she was weighing it up, deciding if she wanted to know more.

'Will you be working with someone called Gaynor?'

Damn Elaine and why do bloody women have to tell each other everything! 'I can't tell you exactly who I'll be working with. I think I can make a real difference though, and I'll need to concentrate on the job.'

He might be able to fool others but his expression had given her the real answer to her question. So not only could his life be in danger, but he'd be working with an ex-girlfriend. She would have to trust him and his next words helped.

'You know you don't have to worry about other women, Mouse. I love you and you are the only one for me.'

The kiss that followed did a lot to alleviate her fears, but received a series of tuts and dirty looks from two of the older German diners.

'And I love you too. I'll be thinking about you every moment you're away.' She leaned over and nuzzled his ear.

'Will you promise me something?' Guy put down his cutlery and took both her hands in his. He looked so earnest that it made her heart melt.

'Anything.'

'Will you try to keep out of trouble please?' He meant no repeats of the business with KC.

'That chapter of my life is most definitely over,' said Mouse, who was on the same wavelength. 'But I can't do anything about it if he turns up at my unit.'

'I know that but...'

'He'd be totally stupid to do that now and it would ruin his boxing career too. I don't think we have any worries there.'

And she really believed it.

Chapter 14

KC loved his boxing and was in peak physical condition. He still accompanied some of his work mates to the Rheindahlen discos on a few occasions, purely to discover whether this would be the best place to exact his revenge on Mouse. It had been quite easy to go unnoticed in the dark, surrounded by tipsy or drunken soldiers and civvies. He ensured he didn't sit in one place for too long and if any of the men he accompanied drew attention to themselves, he quietly moved away until the attention focussed elsewhere. It would have been the ideal place to get her on her own, but the trouble was she hadn't been there the three times that he had. He'd have to find another way but knew he couldn't risk breaking into her accommodation block like before. The security had been improved but he also had a life and there was too much to lose.

As he looked around, a woman approached. He didn't like the look of her and was about to tell her to *do one*.

'We have something in common.'

KC said nothing. She looked at his drink and ordered him another pint, and one for herself. After licking some of the froth and taking a swig, she returned her glass to the bar.

'That bitch Mouse Warbutton needs to learn a lesson,' she could see that she had his attention. 'And between us, we can show her, once and for all.' KC lifted his drink and smiled. They chinked glasses and turned to face the dance floor, partners in crime. Moira Jones had guessed he'd do anything to exact revenge on his ex – exactly as she'd hoped.

*****

After a few months in Northern Ireland the new operators had settled into the routine of the job. Guy entered the pub with his partner and they sat at the table nearest the door. It was raining and their clothes were wet and smelled damp and dank. It's always bloody raining he thought as he focussed his attention on the other customers. Escaping the heavy showers had given them the excuse they needed to go into the pub. A number of other people seemed to have had the same idea. Guy gave Gaynor a peck on the check and walked to the bar to order their drinks. All of the operators were able to mimic the local accent and with his casual clothes and long hair, nobody gave Guy a second look. He'd already clocked the two suppliers sitting at a corner table. They were dry so must have been there for a while, waiting for their customers he believed. Returning to the table with the drinks the couple clocked the suspected terrorists as soon as they entered the pub. Fifteen minutes later they finished their drinks and quietly left. Gaynor radioed their findings to the Operations Room and was told that once the suspects left the pub, they were to follow and to keep the other call signs informed. On this task they were working with four other operators, two in a car parked a few hundred metres away and the other two on foot. The suspects were small fry and the bosses wanted them in custody, where they'd be more valuable than if they were lying in a morgue. But only if the operators' lives weren't in danger - if they had to shoot they would, and they never shot to injure. If the operation was successful the two suspects would end up in custody either facing long sentences or exchanging information for a shorter period of incarceration. If the latter they'd eventually be relocated and given new identities.

It started to drizzle again so Guy grabbed Gaynor's hand and they crossed the road then walked up it for a bit, heading for the empty bus shelter. The rain turned the daylight grey, which matched the few buildings in the area. The only colour that broke up the drabness was the Republican slogans and graffiti on the walls. They laughed and touched each other as one or two people passed, looking like an ordinary loved-up couple. There were few people about but those that were hardly gave them a second glance in their rush to escape the miserable drizzle. Still able to see the pub, Gaynor watched as the suspects exited and turned left. After discreetly radioing the team, she put her head on Guy's chest, and faced right so she could monitor their progress. Guy always had the feeling that she enjoyed this part of the job more than she should. He had confronted her during their down time but she'd professed her innocence. This wasn't the time to think about anything other than the mission and Guy doubled his concentration. Gaynor's head was now hidden from view and she was able to report the progress without raising any suspicion. They left the bus shelter and followed the suspects for a few minutes, firstly at a distance. A radio message followed shortly after letting them know where the contact was to take place. They made eye contact and Gaynor nodded toward the next corner. Having worked together for long enough Guy didn't need to be told her intention.

They would unholster their weapons ready for action. As Gaynor took a step around the corner, Guy's radio alerted him.

'Golf, Charlie one and two no longer visual.'

It was only a feeling, but Guy had learnt to listen to his gut. If he was wrong they'd laugh about it later, but if he was right he could save her life. Guy launched himself at Gaynor as she turned the corner, simultaneously withdrawing his pistol from his jacket. As rounds whizzed past he knew he'd made the right decision. Now on the hard concrete he rolled to the side, steadied himself, and fired. The first round hit the man in the chest and as he crumpled, the second got him in the head. He was dead by the time he hit the ground. Gaynor had recovered her composure and was now standing. She'd quickly drawn her pistol, which she aimed at the other terrorist. The man looked terrified and kept shouting *don't shoot.* His hands were already raised above his head.

'Lie down, spread your arms and legs, and shut the fuck up.' He followed Gaynor's instructions. She searched him, removing two firearms and a knife, while Guy radioed the Ops Room and other team members.

A number of vehicles arrived shortly after, two other members of their team, paramedics, and a patrol of regular soldiers in uniform. The paramedics confirmed that Charlie one was dead and the body was taken away in the ambulance. The other terrorist was unceremoniously pushed into the rear seat of a Ford Cortina, with a jacket covering his head. The vehicle disappeared. Guy and Gaynor introduced themselves to the regular soldiers using their pseudonyms, and explained what had happened. They then cleared the area and returned to their base, both still waiting for the low following the adrenaline rush. To add to Gaynor's emotional discomfort she found it increasingly difficult to hide her real feelings for Guy, especially now that he'd saved her life.

The action had taken place in a disused industrial area and the weather was too bad for the usual crowds. They were therefore confident their identities hadn't been compromised, and could continue in their undercover roles.

*****

Graham had settled into his new unit in Celle. More used to driving trucks and working with soldiers than officers, he didn't enjoy his job as a staff car driver where he was the personal driver of a judge. The judge was based in Germany permanently and one

151

of his main tasks was chairing court martials. When he wasn't working Graham spent every spare minute either with Grace or in support of her parents, and was willing to endure his job for the time being, until she was moved back to the UK. It had been a slow, hard slog but he could be as stubborn as Grace and she had finally come to accept that he loved her, whether she could walk or not. Her arms were firm and strong now and she could handle her wheelchair with ease. Her doctors believed there was still some room for improvement before Grace left the hospital so Graham expected to remain in Germany for the next couple of weeks at least. He wondered if the time might be right to raise the subject of marriage. Grace might well turn him down again but he was convinced she would eventually say yes. He knew without doubt that she loved him and his love for her was unwavering. Mouse was visiting the weekend after next so he decided to pop the question then. He set about writing a formal letter to Grace's father and planned to inform her parents the day before he proposed.

*****

Some of the operators were coming to the end of their current tour, a few others had one last job to do. They hadn't been getting on. She'd had enough and had requested a training role in England, which had been approved. This was Gaynor's final job with the Det for this tour and she couldn't wait to leave.

She was too professional to let her concentration waiver as they watched in uncomfortable silence when their target disappeared from sight. They would have to leave the car and follow on foot. They didn't like to leave one of their vehicles unattended in a hard area, but had no choice. It wasn't unusual for a surveillance not to go to plan, but Gaynor still felt uncomfortable. She radioed two of the team and received confirmation that they had eyes on their man. She then received a message from the Ops Room. Their involvement in the surveillance was now over and they were to pull out or risk the possibility of their cover being compromised. They made their way back to the car in silence. A crowd had started to gather and both felt uneasy. Knowing how quickly a situation could turn nasty in this location they resisted the urge to run, believing that nobody in the crowd knew who they were and what they were doing. Eyes on the car, from a distance everything looked the same as they'd left it.

Gaynor unlocked the door and they got in. She had wanted to clear the air but this wasn't the time and place. Eager to leave, she didn't check the rear-view mirror so missed some of the crowd moving quickly away. 'This is it then,' she said hurriedly, looking straight ahead as she turned the key in the ignition.

Those were Gaynor's last words as the explosion blew them both to smithereens. What remained of the car was engulfed in flames. The small crowd dispersed as soon as they heard the sirens.

*****

Mouse had taken a call from the COMCEN informing her that an immediate signal required collection. She was happy to leave the office to go and get it. It could be anything from the death or serious injury of a soldier, their dependant, or a relative back in the UK. It could also be a serious incident causing major injury but Mouse doubted this because a number of branches would have been notified and the headquarters would be buzzing. Whatever it was, it was bound to be bad news. She was complacent. This was just a normal day in the office and she had learnt to detach herself emotionally from the grief and bad news of others; it was the only way she could cope with it. She had worked longer hours since staff had been sacked, they all had. His replacement could arrive any day, but until then it would be pretty much flat out. She hoped that the conversation she'd overheard between the boss and the colonel meant the new staff sergeant would be a friendly face. Major Best had asked her to make the brews when Lieutenant Colonel Greaves had popped in for a quick chat. She had deliberately taken her time to put the mugs, sugar bowl and milk jug on the table and had innocently asked if they'd like her to serve the tea. Major Best said they'd manage but she had heard enough of the conversation to know that Sergeant Waters was due promotion and, thought Lieutenant Colonel Greaves, would make a good fit for the G1 Compassionate Cell. He ticked all the boxes as far as Mouse was concerned; genuinely happily married, easy going, intelligent and firm but fair, plus nothing pervy about him! She could only hope that he would be selected for promotion. In the meantime she had an important signal to collect. Grateful for an excuse to leave the office and clear her head for five minutes, she decided to pop to the NAAFI shop while out of the office to buy chocolate for the boss and the other staff. A little treat went a long way and it would be a good morale boost.

Back in the office Mouse dispensed the chocolate while Frau Mueller made the brews. Major Best joined her in the clerical outer office for a quick break. She opened up the envelope while he chatted. There were a number of priority signals there as well as the immediate. She started reading the most important first. It was a NOTICAS - notifiable casualty - and Mouse wondered why they had received the signal notifying them of a female soldier's death, when the woman's parent unit was in the UK. As one part of her brain carried on reading to discover that the servicewoman's parents were in Germany because her father was an OC of a squadron up country, another started to register the woman's name and remember where she'd heard it before.

Major Best stopped eating as he saw the colour drain from her face. 'Man the phones please,' he said to Frau Mueller. And tell Corporal Roper we're not to be disturbed. Frau Mueller left and Major Best closed the door. He took the signal from her shaking hands and read.

'Is he working with her, Corporal Warbutton?' he asked.

'He wouldn't confirm it, but from his reaction I know he was meant to be working with a girl called Gaynor who was an ex-girlfriend.' Her voice was a whisper as the tears started running down her cheeks. Even in her distress, she had no intention of telling her boss that Elaine had uncovered the information through her RMP network.

Who he was working with was classified information and on a *need to know* basis. Even knowing how innovative she was, Major Best was still surprised and impressed that she had managed to discover this information. He hid his feelings deciding not to mention it; now wasn't the time. The signal said that there were two of them in the car and it didn't look good. They only needed to know the name of the soldier whose next of kin were under their area of responsibility. As well as a NOTICAS, it was a PUBLINCTCAS – of interest to the public – so in the UK, a Ministry of Defence public information team would be trying to limit the information given to the press. It was time for Major Best to call in a favour. The best thing he could do for her was to obtain the facts so she would know, one way or another.

'Let's go into my office.' He eased her up from the chair by the elbow and Mouse followed him, in a dreamlike state. She

154

was trembling by the time he led her to an easy chair and she put her head in her hands as Major Best dialled a number.

Surely if Guy was dead she would have felt something thought Mouse as she sat waiting. It was as if she were somebody else, looking at this poor distressed girl waiting to discover whether her man was still alive. Mouse thought about all the silly arguments they'd had but mostly about the last time they'd made love and how they both knew they were soul mates, and meant to be together. Somewhere in the background she also listened to Major Best's conversation.

'Right, Barry. I'm on my way round now.' He listened to the voice on the other end of the phone then continued. 'Yes, I know I owe you one.' He hung up and hurried out of the office. A few seconds later he returned with Frau Mueller. 'I'm going to G2 Security to use their secure phone, Mouse. I have a contact.'

She knew he'd be as quick as he could but the wait was unbearable. As Mouse closed her eyes and prayed silently to a God she hadn't believed in until now, Frau Mueller held her hands and whispered words of comfort. Some were in English and others German. Mouse didn't care, she needed to be with someone and Frau Mueller's presence stopped her from losing control.

Major Best returned shortly after and gave her the news. The tension left her body and Mouse sobbed until she could cry no more.

She was no good to man or beast and Major Best told her to go. Knowing she shouldn't be left on her own, he arranged for Spike to be with her.

*****

The sad news of the deaths was on Forces television that night, but the names of the casualties had not yet been released. KC listened with interest then made a call to a one of his boxing team mates who worked in the COMCEN. His mate was entirely unprofessional and broke all the rules by telling him about Gaynor's death. Moira Jones phoned the block and KC hurried to take the call. She told him that Mouse was distressed and had been sent home from work, accompanied by a friend. KC put two and two together and convinced himself that her boyfriend was the other one who'd been killed. He felt no sympathy and reverting to type, rubbed his hands in glee. He hoped it was him and knew that Mouse would be in bits. That would teach the bitch.

Knowing the grief she would be going through should have been enough for KC but it wasn't. He wanted to witness her suffering. The following day, a Saturday, he drove to JHQ.

Still in shock after the previous day's news, Mouse needed to clear her head. Walking usually did the trick. Despite Spike's desire to accompany her, she insisted on going alone. She needed to think about her future, it was daytime and they lived in a safe area. It was a chilly day with patchy clouds in the distance threatening rain, so she set off at a brisk pace. She headed towards the Wegberg hospital gate where she could exit the camp and be in the countryside not much later. The camp wasn't that far from the Dutch border so the area was pretty flat.

KC parked his car near the accommodation blocks. He'd managed to get another loan and had bought a cheap run around. He looked like a typical squaddie and his car had British Forces Germany number plates so was unlikely to cause any suspicion, even if someone saw him sitting there reading his newspaper. He was trying to pluck up the courage to find a way into the block without being noticed, but was pleasantly surprised when he saw Mouse leaving the accommodation. He'd expected she would be consumed by grief and would not want to leave her bunk during the weekend. This was even better. Waiting until she turned the corner he left his car and followed discreetly. He failed to notice another car pull up.

Mouse shivered. She had a strange feeling but had no idea why. Her mother would have said that someone had walked over her grave. She carried on walking but couldn't shake it off. Looking around she saw a man in the distance too far away to be recognisable. She thought nothing of it, just a squaddie or local civilian going about his business. She convinced herself that after the shock of the previous day it wasn't surprising she felt uneasy. She exchanged pleasantries with the security guard as she exited the gate, and walked along the road heading in the direction of the military hospital. Instead of taking the road left as she neared the hospital, she planned to follow the right bend in the road that would lead to the path into the countryside and wooded area. The wind started to pick up and a heavy cloud blocked out the dull glow of the sun, turning the day to grey for a few minutes. Mouse looked up and tried not to imagine what life would be like without the man she loved. She mentally slapped herself, regained her grip on reality and walked on.

There were few people in this area which made KC wonder whether he should only taunt her, as was his original plan, or if he could get away with something else. Daisy the WRVS woman, and Gloria knew how he really felt about Mouse. And so had her boyfriend but he was now out of the picture. KC smiled to himself, a mean nasty smile that didn't reach his eyes. His hands were his weapons and he knew that if he was to do anything, he would have to silence her once and for all. He would taunt her about Guy's death before arranging for them to meet, a lot sooner than she expected. His thoughts both frightened and excited him and as he closed the distance between them, he was still undecided about what way he would despatch her to her maker. The method wasn't important. That she suffered was.

Mouse hadn't seen anyone, not even the usual dog walkers. She wondered if sensible people had watched the weather forecast and decided to remain indoors. It was becoming decidedly darker and she needed to make the decision whether to carry on and risk getting soaked to the skin, or to turn back and shorten her walk. The eternal optimist, she'd left her waterproof in her bunk, so decided to turn around. As she did so, she noticed the man she'd seen earlier. Had he carried on walking toward her Mouse wouldn't have batted an eyelid. He seemed to jump then change course, alerting her that something was amiss. She tensed as she walked back along the path between the trees.

KC knew she'd clocked him and gave up any pretence of hiding. He looked around. Confident they were the only people about, he leaned back against a tree and folded his arms, waiting for her to approach.

Her fight or flight response kicked in when she recognised him. He'd been on Forces News recently and she'd noticed he was in peak physical condition. She already knew he was into Army boxing. There was no way she could outrun him and he would be much stronger than her. Her best hope would be to try reasoning and perhaps somebody would come to her rescue. Walking towards him Mouse took a deep breath, trying to look more confident than she actually felt. He would expect her to mention the attack, so she needed to put him on the back foot and try to buy some time.

'Hello, KC. Congratulations on winning the boxing.' His smug expression was replaced by one of confusion. *That'll teach the bastard.* 'What brings you to this neck of the woods?' She tried to give the impression that this was a normal conversation with someone she'd met unexpectedly, out on her walk.

He unfolded his arms and started pulling the bark off the tree. Mouse knew he was working himself up, not a good sign.

KC was genuinely confused. *How could she be so fucking chipper when her boyfriend had just died? She must know what had happened. Perhaps she was in denial.* All the words he'd imagined saying to her abandoned him and he was left feeling like a complete prick. He pulled at the bark, not wanting to hit her until he'd witnessed her misery and seen her completely broken.

'He probably knew he was going to die. You know that don't you? But there was fuck all he could do about it. You know there'll be nothing left of your boyfriend to bury? He's already been cremated,' he laughed.

It was now her turn to look confused and she wondered what he was talking about.

'You do know he died in an explosion?'

When she'd seen Gaynor's name on the signal Mouse had thought exactly the same. It was only because the boss had found out they'd stopped working together and Gaynor had a new partner that she knew Guy was safe. Had KC somehow discovered that Guy worked with Gaynor and come to the wrong conclusion? How could he have found out? She wondered for a mili-second whether KC had information that Major Best wasn't privy to, and then dismissed it. KC was an average mechanic at best, who was good with his hands but not his brain. She was convinced that the Army would have got rid of him by now if it wasn't for the boxing. He didn't have the intelligence, personality or leadership abilities to further his career.

'He's alive and well thanks, KC. So you've come here for nothing. Why don't you just get on with your life and leave me alone to get on with mine?'

'He's fucking dead! And nobody does what you've done to me and gets away with it.' He moved toward her.

'But I didn't get away with it. You've already had your revenge. Why can't you just leave it at that?' Knowing she couldn't outrun him, she wondered bizarrely whether she could try to climb a tree and wait until help came.

'He's dead, dead, dead! And you're going to join him, sooner than you think.'

She took one last look into the deranged eyes of her ex-fiancé and knew that he meant it. She ran, terrified, like a fox trying to escape a pack of hounds. If she could get to the road, she would have a better chance than if he caught her in the woods. Knowing that her very life depended on it, Mouse ran with all her heart.

*****

Guy parked his car and checked his reflection in the rear-view mirror. He smoothed down a few stray hairs. Although at the peak of physical fitness he knew he looked like shit. He hadn't slept the night before after hearing about the deaths of Gaynor and Bob, or forty-eight as he remembered Bob from training. Gaynor had formed an unhealthy attachment to him while they worked together. Although they were both consummate professionals, Guy believed that her obvious feelings for him could cause problems and had asked for a new partner. They'd fallen out about it but his request had been approved. He still had a soft spot for her as a mate and also felt guilty. Although shit happened he couldn't help wondering whether they'd be looking for pieces of him to send back to his family instead of Bob, had he still been working with Gaynor. Or, if he would have noticed the crowd dispersing or the IED and stopped her from turning the key. But if Gaynor and Bob hadn't suspected anything, why would he?

It brought the fragility of life home to him and dispelled any doubt about what Guy wanted from his future. He knew he wanted to marry Mouse as soon as possible. He also knew that she might put two and two together if she watched the news so was desperate to let her know that he was OK. Or, he corrected himself, as OK as he could be after terrorists had just murdered two of his mates. He picked up the bunch of flowers from the passenger seat and made his way to the block. A few minutes later he returned to his car. Spike had told him she hadn't been gone long and gave him the general direction in which Mouse usually walked. He returned to the car and made his way there.

As Guy exited the camp via the Wegberg hospital exit he could see two figures walking in the distance. Maybe it was his training or perhaps his sixth sense, but his feelings told him the second figure was up to no good. He drove as near to the wooded area as he could, then parked the car and followed on foot. As soon as he was off the road and into the woods he left the main path and took an obvious shortcut, lessening the distance between them.

159

KC enjoyed the chase and it didn't take long for him to catch up. He rugby tackled her and dragged her to the base of a tree. Her efforts to scramble forward were no match for his strength. She was soon out of breath but kept struggling. He grabbed her hair and pulled her head roughly back. Her chest rose and fell rapidly with the effort of her struggle and her world went into slow motion as she realised he planned to batter her head against the tree trunk – strength came from pure fear and she doubled her efforts.

Mouse heard a noise from behind and felt his grip relax. With nothing to struggle against she turned to face him and couldn't believe her eyes. KC was slumped in a heap and smiling down at her was the man she loved.

'Are you all right, sweetheart?'

She laughed. It seemed totally inappropriate.

'Is he dead?'

'No, but he's going to have a sore head when he wakes up.' Guy cuffed KC, confirming that he was unconscious. He pulled Mouse up and she collapsed onto him. He closed his eyes for a second, breathing in the apple scent of her hair, while trying to stop her from shaking.

'Mouse?'

'I'm going to be fine, Guy. I'm home.' He knew exactly what she meant.

Chapter 15

Both on leave, they decided to spend part of the break in Germany and the rest in the UK. Guy had already booked a cottage in the Lake District. They needed some time alone, without any outside distractions. Mouse had decided to cook their first proper meal after an enjoyable but windy day walking through the beautiful countryside. Wine and beer were cooling in the fridge while Mouse boiled the kettle for the Smash instant potatoes. Guy watched in horror as she tried her best to batter the lumps out of the potato mix. In doing so she forgot about the pork chops and smoke billowed from the grill.

'Shit!' Mouse dropped the grill as she burnt her hand on the handle. The already ruined chops splattered across the tiled floor.

'I can salvage this,' she said as she attempted to stir the baked beans, which were now stuck to the inside of the saucepan.

Guy turned off the heat under the grill and saucepan, then ran the cold water, gently putting her hand under it. He caught her eye and they burst out laughing. 'Good job you're a career woman eh?'

She turned off the tap and put her arms around his neck. The cold water dribbled down the back of his shirt, but he didn't care. They locked lips for a long, lazy kiss.

'Chippy?' said Guy when they eventually came up for air.

'Yes please.'

'Will you marry me, Mouse?'

'You know I will.'

'I mean soon, I don't want to wait any longer.'

'Only if you bring me a steak and onion pie with a large portion of chips.'

'It's a deal.' He picked up the car keys. 'Think you can manage to butter some bread by the time I return?' A cushion bounced off the door as he closed it behind him.

*****

It was Graham's turn.

Grace was having one of her good days. She'd had physiotherapy and was tired but was dressed and sitting up in her wheelchair talking to him, when her parents arrived. Sensing something was in the offing, she turned to Graham.

'What's going on?'

'A little surprise for you, darling, that's all.' Her mother answered and Mouse walked in with Guy at the same time. Grace was delighted to see them and squeezed Mouse until she squealed. 'Lighten up, Grace. You're going to kill me.'

'Sorry. I forgot how strong I've become.' She noticed straight away how happy they looked. Mouse was practically glowing. 'What have you two been up to? Any news for us?'

Graham could see that if he didn't do something soon, they would steal his thunder. He gave an unnatural cough and all heads turned to him.

'That's not the only surprise, Grace.'

She had an idea of what was coming, and tried to keep her face neutral, but failed as he knelt on one knee in front of her chair.

'Grace Fleming. Will you do me the honour of becoming my wife?'

She said nothing and Graham's heart missed a beat as he watched a few tears travel slowly down her cheeks. *Oh shit, she's going to say no.*

He wasn't going to give up that easily. 'Marry me, Grace?' He removed the box from his pocket and opened it, displaying the ring with a tiny, exquisite diamond. 'We can change it if you don't like it.'

'Oh, Graham. Yes I'll marry you, and yes I love it!'

He placed the ring on her finger and as he stood up, Grace launched herself at her new fiancée, flinging her arms around his neck. The momentum took them forward and Graham bore all her weight. He forgot about the other visitors for a minute as he twirled her around before they kissed. It was now her father's turn to cough, feigning embarrassment.

'How about a double wedding?' said Guy. They'd discussed it on the way over, knowing that Graham was going to propose. Mouse was all for it. She didn't relish the thought of being the centre of attention and knew that Grace felt the same, especially since being in a wheelchair that she wasn't one hundred per cent comfortable with.

'Grace?'

'That's a fantastic idea, Graham. If everyone else is up for it, let's do it.'

Her father opened the bedside cabinet and produced a bottle of champagne and some plastic glasses. 'I think this calls for a celebration.'

Epilogue

Sitting on his bunk in his cell, KC had plenty of time to think about his bad life choices. He'd received a dishonourable discharge and nine months in civvy nick. He'd hoped to be a model prisoner but that hope had gone out of the window when he'd defended himself against a poof who'd wanted a piece of him. Already sporting a black eye, he was glad that boxing, the one thing he had done really well in the Army, might be his only saving grace while doing his time. After everything that had happened, he still blamed Mouse for his downfall and spent his days obsessed with thoughts of how he'd make her pay. And pay she would when he got out.

Acknowledgements

Thanks to my husband Allan for his love and support, to my editors Philip McAllister-Jones and Rachel Crawford (her books are awesome) and to Trudy Eitschberger, Julie Woodruff and Katie Fleming. Thanks also to Tina and Stuart Graham for providing the research material (and anecdotes) about the Falkland Islands (Stuart was a former *SO2 Penguins* in the Falkland Islands so knows his stuff).

While the characters in this book are purely fictitious, most of the events and places, with the exception of special duties training and Northern Ireland, are based on my own reality or that of someone I know. The majority of my research regarding special duties training is from the excellent book 'The Operators' by James Rennie.

Author's Note

Thank you for purchasing this book. I hope you enjoyed reading it as much as I did writing it. I'd be very grateful if you'd consider leaving a review on Amazon. If you'd like to hear about my new book releases you can subscribe at this link buff.ly/23GU3va and receive a free copy of 'Jason the Penguin' suitable for three to eight year olds.

Printed in Poland
by Amazon Fulfillment
Poland Sp. z o.o., Wrocław